"You must choose my victim," repeated the vampire. He smiled. The teeth slid over his lips and touched his chin. "Although you have not discussed the issue as I requested, I think you all know, if you consider it for a moment, who has caused the most trouble here."

Sherree nodded. Without the slightest hesitation, she said, "I nominate Lacey." Sherree was calm. Relaxed. She was comfortable with her decision.

Sherree's calm spread through the tower just as the vampire's stench had. Bobby's mind seemed to return. Zach's trembling lessened. Randy's terror dwindled. Roxanne's anger quieted.

"Lacey," repeated the vampire, as if tasting the syllables before he tasted the victim. *"Lacey."*

Sherree is giving me to him, thought Lacey.

She was unable to believe it. She had been sure they would stick together as a group. But no. Darwin was correct. Survival of the fittest. What it meant was — throw out one member to save the rest.

Also in the Point Horror series:

Point Horror

THE VAMPIRE'S PROMISE

Caroline B. Cooney

SCHOLASTIC

Scholastic Children's Books,
Scholastic Publications Ltd,
7-9 Pratt Street, London NW1 0AE

Scholastic Inc.,
730 Broadway, New York, NY 10003, USA

Scholastic Canada Ltd,
123 Newkirk Road, Richmond Hill,
Ontario, Canada L4C 3G5

Ashton Scholastic Pty Ltd,
P O Box 579, Gosford, New South Wales,
Australia

Ashton Scholastic Ltd,
Private Bag 1, Penrose, Auckland,
New Zealand

First published by Scholastic Inc. 1993
This edition published by Scholastic Children's Books 1993

ISBN 0 590 55381 X

Printed by Cox & Wyman Ltd, Reading, Berks

10 9 8 7 6 5 4 3 2

THE VAMPIRE'S PROMISE

Chapter 1

Lacey was the first to realize that a vampire shared the dark with them.

"What's that smell?" she said. She already knew. The knowledge seemed to have been born in her centuries ago, waiting for this single moment, this particular evening, this very darkness, to emerge. Somewhere, in another life, in another country, she had smelled this before.

A low growing mold, like an ancient cellar with a dirt floor.

The smell began beneath Lacey's feet and rose up around her like swamp gas.

She already knew it was too late to run, and that even if she could run, she could not escape.

Her sneakers were flimsy and light, pretty little summer canvas shoes, bought to last a few weeks and then be discarded. She tried to take a step, but the rubber soles stayed where they were, as if she were caught up to the ankles in sucking mud.

In the queasy darkness of the old building, the sneakers no longer seemed bright pink with white laces. They had taken on a dank and soiled look, as if something had been drained over them.

"Do you smell that?" whispered Lacey.

But nobody else did, because Roxanne, dressing for the evening, had splashed her new perfume on her throat and wrists; and because Zach, always on the verge of starvation, had opened the popcorn. Popcorn and perfume lay on separate levels in the room, and beneath them, the smell of the vampire rose like dirty fingers.

It was early fall. Still warm out. Lacey was wearing a white cotton dress silkscreened with golden wildflowers. Lacey felt on display. As if she really were a golden wildflower, and the vampire a honeybee. He would see her colors. And then, a moment later, he would be aware of her scent, as she was aware of his.

The silly teenage laughter and the popcorn munching of the others in the room bounced on the surface of the terrible smell.

Lacey breathed deeply to calm herself, to slow her pounding heart and ease her cramped lungs, but the smell overwhelmed her. She could hardly bear to breathe at all. She could feel the soft pink of the insides of her lungs being contaminated by the vampire's smell, like miners breathing in coal dust.

Perhaps that's how it works, she thought. Perhaps you suffocate yourself. You pass out. You don't feel anything when he stoops over you. You don't even know what's happening until it's too late.

Lacey trembled in the middle of the dark room.

He is here for me, she thought.

How could she have been so foolish as to wear cotton summer clothing? Every inch of her flesh was vulnerable. She needed more. She needed to be wrapped in something. A long leather coat. High boots. Certainly a thick collar or a tightly wound scarf on her neck.

The electricity had been cut off months ago.

The old mansion had no power. No lights.

Of course, that had been the point: to party in the dark. To frighten themselves. Make the night long and panicky.

It was a time-honored tradition among teenagers.

Randy had almost been embarrassed to suggest it, because it was trite. Overdone. The old party-in-the-abandoned-house trick.

But everyone he had invited had come.

And to his shame, they were not the ones who were afraid.

Randy was.

Although the house was darker than any place Randy had ever been — no moon, no stars, no streetlights, no headlights, no houselights — Randy saw something even darker.

A piece of the dark darkened more, like gauze becoming velvet, and then it moved toward him.

It was like seeing wind.

Seeing that wind swirl, and turn on itself, and suck up the dust.

It was a cape without a person inside.

Randy's short hair stood up vertically, like a cat on a fence. He sat on the floor, cross-legged, a handful of popcorn in one hand and a can of Pepsi in the other, while the vampire slowly filled out his cape.

A hand that was more bone than flesh came first. It flexed itself, and fingernails grew from the tips: crinkled and split like torn foil. Its skin was the color of mushrooms. The hand caught the edge of the darkness and tucked it in tighter: it could make a cape out of the very air in the room.

And finally, the teeth were visible. Teeth that hung over thin lips like stakes on a picket fence. The teeth even peeled like fence posts in need of paint.

But it was not paint these teeth needed.

Randy had wanted an adventure.

He had not thought of this one.

Lacey backed away, trying to find the door.

She had been very silly to agree to this dumb adventure. Very, very silly to lie to her parents about where she would be; when she would get home; whom she would be with.

Time to go. Yes, definitely, time to end this party.

"I possess the door," said the vampire. His voice spread through the room like a groping, rising tide and then just lay there, quivering.

He was correct. Though the door was open, and the stairway to freedom beckoned below it, the air was solid. Lacey was not going anywhere.

The backs of her eyes and her neck grew cold, as if she were being anesthetized.

Perhaps she was.

Perhaps she was to be the first.

She was the only one standing. The rest at least were sitting near each other, could hold hands, could have the strength that only a group can give.

Lacey whimpered and the vampire smiled, courteously covering his teeth.

Roxanne had been thinking that it was time to dump Bobby. It had been fun, running around with a younger boy, but senior year was moving right along, and Roxanne had to think in terms of the prom. She certainly wasn't going with Bobby. So far, her friends thought it cute and funny that she would dabble in tenth-graders, so to speak. But if it lasted much longer, she would just seem weird, and Roxanne did not wish to cross that line.

Roxanne had been sitting on the floor playing with her hair. She had been growing it out forever and ever, and it was finally below her shoulders, but now that she had it, she couldn't stand it. Long hair was such a pain. She was ready to cut it short again. Shorter than even the boys wore their hair. She wanted a new persona: sharp, bright, vivid, demanding. No more of this sweet romantic stuff.

Roxanne wanted to make waves. Astonish people. Set trends.

She flipped up her hair, making a pretend ponytail, and twisting the handful of hair tightly on top of her head.

On her bare neck, a queer cold finger pressed down.

But whose finger? She could see all the others. Old dwindle-head Lacey, standing alone. Silly cheerleader Sherree, doing what she did best, giggling between Randy and Bobby. Zachary, lip curled in an above-it-all sneer, attracting Roxanne so much she could hardly stand it.

There was nobody whose hand could touch her neck.

But the hand remained.

And a terrible voice, slimy with mud or entrails, said, "I possess the door."

Randy had promised everybody that this would be a night to end all nights. The six teenagers were motionless, unbreathing, unwilling to show fear. They were waiting for Randy to show them this was a trick, an event staged for their amusement.

The pressure on Roxanne's neck ceased.

The cape, empty, circled the six.

Within it, the hand, the feet, and the face came and went.

When the vampire spoke again, they knew it was not a staged event. "I was asleep," said the vampire reproachfully.

"I'm sorry we came," said Randy. He found that he had crushed the popcorn in his fist. Salty buttered crumbs covered his palm. "It's my fault," he said quickly, hoping to make peace. "We'll leave."

The vampire shook his head. "Now that I'm up," said the vampire, "I am quite hungry, you see."

They could see. It was very dark in the tower of the old house, and yet the vampire reflected his own light, just as he swirled in his own wind and stank with his own odor.

"We're trespassing," said Bobby, as if acknowledging the crime made it okay. He was the bright confident voice of the jock, the emerging and coddled school star, the one who could get away with anything. "We'll leave you in peace."

The vampire smiled, and this time did not bother to cover his teeth. "I've had enough peace for this decade," said the vampire. "I don't believe I am interested in peace tonight."

Lacey wondered how long her knees would continue to hold her up.

The teeth seemed to grow even as she watched, white fangs over which a sort of moss hung.

The six teenagers looked down at their own skin, largely bare in their skimpy summer clothing. How precious their skin seemed. How pale. Phosphorescent, almost, as if they had dunked themselves in some neon mixture prior to the party.

"You were showing off," the vampire said to Randy, shaking his head regretfully.

"I'm sorry," whispered Randy. "I won't do it again."

The cloak rasped like dried leaves, and it shed, like a scattering of evil herbs. "That is true," agreed the vampire. He smiled immensely, a politician, perhaps, who knew nobody could vote against him.

"Boys," said the vampire meditatively. "Boys have to press the accelerator to the floor. They have to drink harder and kick footballs farther. It is never enough for a boy to *know* that he is quicker than the rest. A boy has to prove it, and he has to prove it over and over and over again."

The cloak fell back and they could see more of him now, musty and unused. Undercooked.

"Nothing is more dangerous than a boy aged sixteen," said the vampire. It seemed to be a favorite subject of his. "Their parents know it. The insurance companies know it. A sixteen-year-old boy is a pulsating envelope of desire to show off. The only ones who don't know it are the boys. They think what they're doing is perfectly reasonable."

Good, thought Roxanne, the rest of us are all right. It's Randy he wants. Randy brought us here and the vampire is going to make him pay for that. Relief flooded Roxanne.

"You were showing off," said the vampire to Randy. He shook a long, thin index finger at Randy. The fingernail glittered like crushed aluminum.

Randy said he was sorry. Randy said he would never show off again. Randy said they would clean up and get out.

Parents were always on your case to clean up. It was a plan with which they were all well acquainted: cleaning up their act. The six began reaching around, grabbing soda cans and popcorn bags and the portable radio, trying to leave the house with no trace of themselves.

"I'm awake now," said the vampire. "And I'm not sorry at all, Randy. I believe I'm quite happy about it."

He did not look happy. He was smiling, of course, but with those teeth, it was not a pleasant smile.

"Suppose," said the vampire, "that I leave you for a while." He looked deep into the eyes of each of them.

Roxanne let go of her ponytail and massaged the back of her neck.

Sherree and Zachary flinched.

Even Bobby shivered.

Tears crawled down Lacey's cheeks.

Randy found that he had bent the antenna of his radio into a U.

"While I am gone," said the vampire, "you will have an important discussion."

We will run, thought Bobby, who was in splendid physical condition. No zombie fresh out of the grave was a match for him. Bobby eyeballed the distance to the stairs. He'd make it. He didn't know about the others. He didn't care about the others.

Only Lacey, still standing, knew that they could not go anywhere. The open door was solid with the vampire's atmosphere.

"I will let five of you go in safety," said the vampire. He was beginning to laugh. He was not simply hungry for blood. He was hungry for entertainment.

"You will choose who among you is to satisfy my hunger," said the vampire. "That person will stay with me. Here. In the dark. In the quiet of this tower."

Sherree began to sob.

The vampire smiled appreciatively. His eyes assessed their necks. "The person you choose . . ." he said, lingering on every syllable, "and I . . ." he said, lisping through his teeth, ". . . will have much to occupy us."

He withdrew his teeth, tucking them slowly behind his lips. They hardly fit. He dried his mouth with the edge of his dark cloak.

The vampire said, "I will still be here, of course. The door will remain mine. But I won't listen in on your little talk. That wouldn't be fair."

He disappeared quite slowly, folding himself up in his cloak.

His smell stayed after him.

Chapter 2

When Randy had suggested breaking into the Mall House with the girls and spending the night there, he thought he was being clever. Randy needed to show off more than most boys because he hated his name. Randy was such a weak-kneed name. He wanted to be named Bobby, which sounded relaxed and strong, or Zach, which sounded successful and quick, but those were the names of his two best friends. Bobby and Zach were somehow always ahead of Randy. Not by much, but by enough.

And whenever Randy was the first to think of something, Bobby and Zach were the first to tell him how dumb his idea was.

"The Mall House?" said Bobby. "That pathetic old mansion with the broken shutters?" Bobby was a sophomore, Randy and Zach juniors. But Bobby had always seemed older than Randy because he was always in a position of honor, winning games and trophies for every team.

"The Mall House?" said Zach, laughing. Nobody could laugh with such scorn as Zach. "Come on,

Randy. They stripped the place of anything valuable years ago."

Actually it had been only a year ago that the last occupants had moved out. A weird family. Not that anybody normal had ever lived in the mansion. There were stories about a girl named Althea who'd moved away before Randy was in high school. The mansion had been vacant for a while. And then Devnee's family had moved in. Randy remembered her clearly. A girl he had found plain at the beginning of the school year, captivatingly beautiful during the middle, and ordinary again toward the end. He had never figured out what she had done to herself to metamorphose like that. But Devnee's family, too, had left town. Vanished.

Nobody seemed to enjoy living in the mansion.

"It's just waiting for the wrecking ball," said Zach in his most put-down voice. "I heard they're finally pulling it down next week." Zach always had facts nobody else had.

"Right," said Randy. "If we're gonna do it, we've gotta do it now."

"Why," asked Zach, "would we want to do it at all?" Zach was thin and languid and took his time at everything, from schoolwork to sports, and yet still he managed to ace and to win. Sometimes Randy worshipped Zach and sometimes he hated him. This was a hating time.

"Because the girls would be scared," said Randy.

Bobby yawned, affecting mild amusement that his friend was so immature he'd rather scare a girl than kiss her. "Come on, Randy," said Bobby. "We stopped scaring girls when we were twelve."

In Bobby's case this was actually true. There was nobody in the entire school system as socially advanced as Bobby. Bobby was the kind of guy who wore a neon-green baseball cap, backward, and still looked cool. In sixth grade he had had ninth-grade girls flirting with him and now that he was in tenth, seniors were falling at his feet.

Bobby just jogged off the playing field and made a choice among the eager females waiting on the sidelines. This year, incredibly, Bobby made not one choice but two. He was not only dating Roxanne, a beautiful and brilliant senior, but also Sherree, a bubble-bath-cute ninth-grader. Bobby would alternate Sherree and Roxanne, and either Sherree and Roxanne didn't notice, or they adored Bobby so much they didn't mind. Randy kept expecting a nursery rhyme situation in which the calico cat and the gingham dog would eat each other up, but no. Each girl linked arms with Bobby when it was her turn and stayed friends.

As for Zachary, he did not date. He said this was because he had high standards, and local girls simply did not meet them. Bobby said Zach did not date because Zach would not participate in anything where he could not get an A plus, and you were never entirely sure whether you'd be an A plus with any girl. It's okay to get a C in class, Bobby told Randy confidentially, but it's really crummy to have a C average in girls.

Both Bobby and Zach felt that going around with Lacey was a C average in girls.

Randy tried to defend his suggestion about partying at the old mansion. "Lacey loves to be scared. We go to amusement parks and she screams on the scary rides, and we go to movies and she screams at the scary parts, and we — "

"Lacey is a dwindle-head," said Zach. "I can't believe you go out with her."

Part of Randy wanted to tell Zach where to go, or beat Zach up and settle it with broken bones. But a larger part of Randy hated himself for dating a girl that Zach considered a dwindle-head. Zach, of course, would never be seen near a dwindle-head.

Randy addressed Bobby instead. "Bring Sherree or Roxanne," said Randy. "Or both. We'll sneak into the house around eleven o'clock, and — "

Bobby laughed out loud. "Randy, get a grip on yourself. Bring Sherree or Roxanne to the Mall House? They'd die first. Those are girls I have to spend money on, huh? Get it? They don't sleep on floors, Randy. And they don't lean back against splintered walls, eating in the dark from a bag of potato chips, and pretending it's fun."

Bobby and Zachary lost interest in Randy. They picked up the slick advertising circular from the biggest video rental place in town and discussed what movies to rent. Did they want chases and archaeology? Or should they concentrate on war and technology? Horror and axes?

Randy's insides knotted with rage. Nothing could be worse than being dismissed. If Bobby and Zach had not turned their backs . . .

But they had.

And so Randy turned his back as well, and left the room — although it was his house; he had the best video center of any teenager in town. In his heart he knew that was why Bobby and Zach hung out with him — for the electronics he provided. Randy went to the telephone.

The rage percolated into courage and he made three phone calls.

Phone calls he would never have made under normal circumstances.

But he was showing off.

And it seemed reasonable at the time . . .

. . . Randy stared at the vampire. It was becoming clear why this mansion had been sold so often.

Lacey did not know that anybody was referring to her as a dwindle-head. She happened to despise Bobby and Zachary, the most conceited idiots in the entire high school, but although Lacey had a strong personality, she would not have been able to laugh it off. Being called a dwindle-head by two such popular boys would hurt.

Lacey had never had a boyfriend before Randy.

Randy made her nervous and unsure, and dating made her very nervous and very unsure. But she wanted to participate; she wanted to be doing what all the songs on all the radio stations said you should be doing — falling in love.

She didn't really love Randy, but she was trying.

She stuffed her head full of love-thoughts, and sat in love-postures, and listened to love-music.

It didn't take.

Randy was just a nice ordinary kid, half twerp and half jock. He was growing in all directions at once, both mentally and physically, and it was hard to keep track of Randy, or know if she even wanted to. She was fond of him, but mostly she was fond of going out.

Lacey felt very guilty over this.

Should you go out with a boy just in order to leave the house and be seen in other places? This seemed mean and low-minded. Lacey was a nice girl and didn't want to be mean or low-minded.

And yet, Randy kept calling her. He must be happy.

On that crucial night a week ago, Lacey had been half hoping he would call. Strange the way a telephone could rule your existence. It had become her center of gravity; she rotated around it like a moon around a planet.

And I don't even love Randy, she thought. I wonder what it's like when you really do love the boy.

She dreamed of love, of the boy she would meet one day, when stars and rockets and fireworks would fill her mind and soul and body.

And when the phone finally did ring, and it was Randy, she felt so guilty for dreaming about somebody better that she was ready to do anything Randy asked.

It took some serious planning to be able to arrange for a Saturday night without parental knowledge of her whereabouts. Lacey was always hearing about unsupervised teens whose parents hadn't

seen them in days and didn't care where they were
or what they were doing, but she, personally, had
never encountered such a parent. All the parents
she knew foamed at the mouth and confiscated car
keys if anybody vanished for even an hour.

It was agreed that Lacey would say she was at
Roxanne's and Roxanne would say she was at Sherree's, and they would all just hope that nobody had
an emergency involving a phone call or they would
be in deep trouble.

Lacey had never been in trouble, or even close
to trouble, and found herself strangely attracted to
the idea of her parents making an ordinary phone
call, finding no Lacey, first being confused, then
furious, then panicked, and finally weeping, wondering, aching with fear and loss.

Well, they would not think of looking for her in
the Mall House.

Lacey's family lived on the far side of town and
didn't have occasion to drive on this road. Her
mother was not of the shop-till-you-drop persuasion
and would not have kept up-to-date on the possibility of a new mall going up where once a decrepit
house had stood.

Nobody had called it the Mall House when it still
had a family living there.

It got the name Mall House when the Zoning
Committee decreed that nobody could rip the place
down because it was An Historic Building and the
would-be builders said, No, it's a Piece of Junk.
For months people argued the pros and cons of this

situation, and the old boarded-up mansion had gotten its nickname.

Wrong nickname, thought Lacey. It's the vampire's house.

The vampire sifted slowly out of sight. Not because he left, but because he ceased to be. She felt his molecules still drifting around the room, like an evaporating perfume. She did not even want to breathe, lest vampire threads clog her lungs.

Sherree had never had a phone call from Randy before. She had to stop and think who on earth this could be. Randy, she had pondered. Do I know a Randy?

Luckily Randy expected her to be confused and he added, "You know. Bobby's friend. You came to my house to see a movie last month."

"Ooooh, yes! You have that fabulous media room, with the carpeted levels and the big soft floor pillows and the little kitchenette full of snacks and sodas right downstairs with the big big big wallscreen. I never saw a screen that big in somebody's house! Sure, I remember your house, Randy."

Sherree did not hear her own sentence. (She never did quite hear what she was saying out loud.) She did not realize how hurtful it was to be told your TV room was easier to remember than you were.

"A sleepover?" said Sherree dubiously. "I don't know, Randy. My parents are pretty strict."

She paid attention to his offer because she paid close attention to anything a boy said. Sherree did not believe there was much worth thinking about except boys. Luckily there were so many of them. Sherree knew perfectly well that Bobby was dating Roxanne at the same time, but Sherree had learned that what boys wanted most was what other boys already had. Going with Bobby was increasing Sherree's desirability, and pretty soon Sherree would extricate herself from Bobby and take advantage of the boys who envied him. She had pretty well decided to wait until after Christmas because a girl who dated Bobby last year said that Bobby was really a big spender in December.

Sherree could not bring Randy's face to mind. Normally her brain was like a huge yearbook of available boys. Why hadn't she registered Randy? Was there something wrong with him or had the rented movies been especially good?

Randy wanted Sherree to pretend that she was really spending the night at a girlfriend's house but he would pick her up and they were going to stay in a haunted house. Bobby and Zach would be there, too.

"A haunted house?" said Sherree. "Give me a break, Randy."

Randy plowed on. The house, he insisted, really was haunted. That was why they were ripping it down. Not because they were going to build a mall there but because of the terrible things that had happened to the human beings who had lived in that house, listened to those banging shutters, climbed those creaking stairs.

"Well . . ." said Sherree.

"We'll have fun," said Randy. "I'll bring the food."

"And movies?" said Sherree. "I love movies."

(Randy had just told Sherree that the house didn't have electricity anymore, but apparently Sherree had drawn no conclusion from this. Perhaps she thought Randy traveled with his own generator.) He said they would have so much fun that they wouldn't need movies. "In fact," Randy said, "I'll bring along a video camera and film us! *We'll* be the movie!"

"Well . . ." said Sherree. "Are there going to be other girls?"

"Of course. Lacey's coming, for one."

Sherree couldn't remember Lacey, either. Randy patiently described Lacey and after she had heard the description three times Sherree felt as if she knew Lacey after all. "Oh, right," said Sherree. "Sure. Lacey. Great."

"Now we don't want lots of people there," warned Randy. "Spoil the fun, you know. So don't tell anybody."

"I won't tell anybody," promised Sherree. She hung up feeling confused. She did not know why they were going to the haunted house, nor quite what they would do once they sneaked in, but Randy seemed very sure of himself.

Sherree wondered what to wear to an event like this. She stood quite happily in front of her closets and bureau drawers, matching and re-matching, thinking maybe she would call this Lacey to see what she was wearing.

The only kind of movie for which Sherree did not have a taste was horror. She never watched those. They were too scary. She could not sleep at night after a horror movie, and if she ever managed to get to bed she had to sleep in fetal position, because she was afraid of what would happen to her toes if they stuck out.

Sherree was wearing sandals and her toes stuck out.

But even without the information she might have gotten from late-night movies, Sherree knew that she did not have to worry about her toes.

The vampire's attention was elsewhere.

And his teeth — his teeth seemed to be everywhere.

They slid in and out of focus, as if lenses on cameras had fogged up.

Sherree tightened herself into a ball, thinking: Lacey's standing up. He'll take her first. I'll run. He can't do two at once.

When the phone rang that night, and it was Randy, Roxanne bit back a laugh. If there was anybody who did not make waves, who did not set trends, and who was not interesting, it was poor Randy. He was the classic case of the kid with the terrific car, the terrific electronics room, and the thick wallet. People hung out with him to use him and Randy had no idea.

Roxanne could not imagine what Randy was talking about, wanting to have a party in a deserted house. Roxanne being Roxanne, she pointed out the flaws in his planning: how they would have to break in, which was illegal; how the police might be called by neighbors; how very possibly the house was structurally unsound and they might fall through a stair tread or otherwise hurt themselves. How, assuming they did get in, a dark house might be interesting for a minute or two, but then what were they going to do?

"Lighten up, Roxanne," said Randy. "There are no neighbors, and back when they built that house, they built 'em to last for centuries. Nothing's broken in there."

"The shutters are," Roxanne pointed out. "It gives me the creeps just to drive by. Especially now, with everything around the place levelled."

The house stuck out of the ground as if it were a growth or a mold. Strange twisted lightning rods stabbed the sky from the peaks of the porch roof and the ugly tower. Bulldozers had razed everything around it, even pulling down the immense dark hedge of towering hemlocks, but the downed trees had never been hauled off. They lay on the ground, dead and brown, a barricade of scaly bark and rotting limbs.

"But what's the point?" said Roxanne. Roxanne's life was filled with master plans. She did not like to undertake anything unless there was a good result from it.

"Something to do," said Randy.

Roxanne's calendar was very full. She did not

need "something" to do. She was willing to rearrange her schedule only if it were something *worthwhile* to do. "But what will we do once we're there?" said Roxanne.

"I'm not telling yet," said Randy.

Roxanne wondered if this was because he had no idea yet.

"I'm just promising," said Randy, "that it'll be a night to end all nights."

And that was a tempting phrase. Roxanne even agreed to help Lacey lie to her parents, although Lacey was about as interesting to Roxanne as dust under the bed. Even after she found out Sherree was going, too, Roxanne stuck with it. It would be an amusing test of Bobby's social abilities: Could he juggle two girls at once? In front of his two skeptical male friends? If the other guests had been people who mattered deeply to Roxanne, perhaps she would not have risked it. But even Bobby had ceased to be at the top of her list. It was her senior year and she was ready to shrug off these younger kids and get back to what counted.

Roxanne looked around the tower.

She looked at the swirling cloak as it waited to learn what human body would be encapsulated within it.

She looked at the five teenagers trapped with her.

One of us must be sacrificed, she thought. One of us has to spend the night with a vampire.

Well, it won't be me.

Chapter 3

Zach was having difficulty pushing the little black lever on his flashlight. He could not seem to make it go forward. His hands were trembling. He, who was always in control of a situation (Zach picked his situations, so he would never be in one he could not control in the first place) could not even control his own fingers.

Zach had to go back quite a few years to remember being afraid. He was often nervous. Zach had high standards. When he entered a class he did it with style. When he made an introduction, he was amusing. When he told a joke, he timed the punch line just right. When he took an exam he got 95. When he went to a party, he was the life of it. He rehearsed all these events; he actually practiced room-entering, sauntering offstage, tie tying, laughing cruelly versus laughing gently. And because it mattered so much to him that he got these details right, Zach was accustomed to being nervous.

But afraid?

Zach frowned, remembering. He had probably been five, because he easily pictured his Halloween costume: He was Superman in a big red cape his older sisters had worn before him, but he had gotten separated from the group, and found himself in a black yard with evilly grinning pumpkins and a skeleton swinging from a tree and spiders cascading off a gutter.

With abject terror he had fallen to the ground. He had not even been brave enough to run. He had not even screamed. He had just collapsed, a little puddle of panic.

He refused ever again to be a little puddle of panic.

Zach controlled his fingers. He got the flashlight on. He moved its rays in a circle around the tower. The light revealed five terrified faces. Nobody was screaming, nobody was even running. They were little puddles of panic.

The vampire was not visible. Either the vampire had told the truth when he said he was not going to stay while they made the decision, or he was composed of a material that did not shine in the dark.

We shouldn't have come up here, Zach thought, furious with himself for making this error. If we'd stayed downstairs . . .

Well, they hadn't.

Zach was having some difficulty planning a strategy. It seemed to take so much more of his energy to hold the flashlight still than this minor physical action should require. His heart was pounding so hard that he did not seem to have much left over for running and escaping.

For the first time, Zach wished he were a jock like Bobby.

Bobby trained for this kind of stuff. All that bench-pressing and lap-running — now it would pay off. Whereas studying for British literature exams — that would get Zach precious little distance from a vampire.

Zach focused the shaft of light on the single open door. Stairs led down to a broad landing on the bedroom floor below the tower, twisted once, and then led down to the old front hall. The teenagers had not, of course, come in the front door. Standing on the old creaking porch, they had peeled back a large slab of plywood that had been nailed over a broken window in the old dining room. Randy had brought along a clawed hammer to pry up the nails.

Zach disliked taking risks without rehearsing them first.

There was quite a bit that could go wrong if he tried to run ahead of the others. Zach flashed the light temptingly out the door and down the tower stairs, hoping one of the others would bolt, and Zach could follow in his wake, let the other guy take the risks for him.

Ever since the vampire had appeared, the tower had been filled with a weird combination of light and dark. There were no lights, and yet Bobby could see himself and the others. The vampire had no color, and no form, and yet Bobby had been able to see him perfectly.

I possess the door, the vampire had said.

Bobby had believed it. The mushroom skin, the dripping fangs, the oozing cloak; it would possess anything it wanted.

But it had evaporated, leaving behind its strange illumination of the tower. And now he believed less. Even a vampire could not possess air, and air was all that could fill the door opening.

Zach leveled the beam of his flashlight on the doorway and Bobby was relieved: The beam passed through the door. If light rays could travel in that space, so could Bobby.

Bobby planned his route.

He was a little worried about stumbling on the stairs. He'd been teasing Roxanne and Sherree so much about things that go bump in the night he had paid no attention to the layout of the house. Once he left here, he'd have to move it; there could be no fumbling on this pass.

Bobby was a player of team sports, but it did not occur to him that perhaps this was a sport and perhaps he had a team with him. He thought only of saving himself as quickly and efficiently as possible.

Bobby took a running start from the back of the tower room and hurled himself forward.

Sherree had never been afraid of anything, either. There was no need. The people around Sherree did everything for her.

Sherree fulfilled the Barbie doll premise: she was incredibly thin, and yet voluptuous. She had masses of fluffy hair and yet none of it ever fell into her oval face. Her eyes were immense, and she wore tinted contact lenses to make them blue-er. She even dressed like a Barbie doll. No skirt was too short, no blouse was too glitzy, no tan was too dark.

Just two weeks ago her car had stopped going while she was driving along some unknown road. She didn't consider for a moment working on the engine, or even wondering what was wrong with it. She simply got out of the car and looked around. It did not surprise Sherree at all that a gas station was only a block away. Its immense sign poked up above the tallest trees, summoning the needy.

Sherree strolled back to the gas station. She had nothing with her but a driver's license; Sherree liked to hold a boy's hand or a steering wheel or both, but she disliked carrying a purse. Consequently she did not have a dime. She couldn't pay for a phone call, let alone a tow or a major repair.

But she did not expect it to be a problem, and it wasn't.

The men at the gas station offered to push her car back to the station to save her the towing fee. All she had had to do was twinkle at them. They let her use their phone to call her father and on Sherree's promise that Daddy would pay, they fixed the car before he arrived.

Twinkling worked.

Sherree had planned to twinkle through all her problems. But she did not want to twinkle at a vampire. The vampire would want her most, because everybody always did. And she was dressed the skimpiest, because Sherree always was.

She knew instinctively that the vampire wouldn't want a boy. That left Roxanne, who was a tough sarcastic type, and Lacey, who was a dwindle-head. They were pretty enough, in their own boring ways, but that was all. I mean really, thought Sherree, what other choices does this vampire have but me?

Sherree assumed that Zach or Bobby would save her.

She did not assume that Randy would. Randy was a little too meager in personality and body to save anybody.

Sherree studied Zach and knew that he was analyzing the situation. She had faith in his brain. He would find a good strategy. She watched Bobby. The athlete drew himself together. He had a fine body, more heavily muscled than most boys his age. No doubt he could rip a T-shirt's sleeves by clenching his biceps. Bobby took a few steps backward, away from the door, gathering himself.

Sherree unwound from her terrified crouch. This was not completely different from cheerleading. You had to bounce up off a gym floor from the most ridiculous positions and leap up. She would spring up and follow Bobby down the stairs.

Bobby turned himself into a battering ram.

Sherree lifted like a sprinter at the starting line.

Bobby flung himself across the tower and plunged through the door.

Except that he did not go through.

He remained in midair. Pinned to the atmosphere like a Velcro wall-jumper. Sherree stared. The door was open, and Bobby was hanging there. Not as if there were a noose around his neck, but as if he were an insect in the vampire's collection, pinned at the joints on the bulletin board.

The vampire indeed possessed the door. And now, clearly, he also possessed Bobby.

Roxanne had the hammer.

Her parents were neatness fanatics; everything in its place. If you left your shampoo bottle on the tub rim, they freaked. If you left a cassette out of its plastic holder, they freaked. If you allowed a used glass to rest on the counter instead of popping it instantly inside the dishwasher, they freaked.

So of course, when the teenagers had gotten into the deserted mansion, and Randy yanked the plywood back to hide the opening he had made, and then absently set the hammer down on the same windowsill they had crawled over, Roxanne picked it up.

They might accidentally leave the hammer behind.

Or not be able to find it again in the dark.

Especially if their flashlight batteries ran down.

It was an ordinary enough hammer, slim wooden handle, hard metal head and claws. She was not wearing a belt in her jeans, so she shoved the handle through a belt loop. It hung satisfyingly against her thigh, making her feel like a tough workman.

When Bobby flew against the vampire's space,

and stuck there, Roxanne found herself wondering if she would have to pry him off with the claws of the hammer.

"Bobby?" said Roxanne stupidly. "Are you okay?"

Bobby said nothing.

"Well," said Zach, in his most maddening, above-it-all preppy voice, "I guess that lets out the door as escape route." Zach actually laughed. "You look a lit-tle strange up there, Bobby, my man."

Bobby said nothing.

In spite of his teasing, Zach had not been amused. In fact, he had been unable to maintain his grip on the flashlight, which he dropped when Bobby smashed into the vampire's space.

The pounding of his heart had increased. He felt like the bass drum in a marching band — he was nothing but a huge reverberating bong. His heart was thrashing around his chest just as Bobby thrashed against thin air.

I'm afraid, thought Zach. He hated himself for it, hated the vampire for causing it, hated the others because they would surely see, and know.

Lacey retrieved the flashlight.

She examined Bobby's predicament. Then she examined Bobby.

Bobby said nothing.

He was stuck there, and yet when she put her own hand into the air around him, she could not feel anything. She had expected to meet resistance. An invisible balloon skin. She groped around Bobby, but could feel no substance from which to peel him away. He was breathing, his lungs swelled beneath her touch, but still he said nothing.

"Eeeuuuhh!" shrieked Sherree. "How can you put your bare hand out there? What if the vampire touches you?"

Lacey shuddered. The vampire was there, of course. No doubt he was taking pleasure in this; it was, after all, the first entertainment he had had in a long time. But somehow she did not think that her hand was going to encounter his slime.

Her hand encountered nothing at all.

Lacey latched her hands around Bobby's waist and pulled, but he did not come free. And he still said nothing. Nothing at all.

The weird thing was how normal it seemed, as if she had often met boys hanging in doorways and knew just what to do next. If you can't pull, try pushing, she reasoned.

So she stepped through the very doorway the vampire supposedly possessed — the doorway Bobby's body had not penetrated — and then turned around to push Bobby back into the tower room.

"You got through!" cried Roxanne, getting up. Roxanne hefted the hammer, ready to split the skull of any vampire that got close to her.

"Run, Lacey!" shouted Randy. He was so proud of her! She was not a dwindle-head after all; he could brag about her now; *now* Bobby and Zach couldn't say anything about Lacey.

But Lacey did not run.

For beyond the door, at the top of the tower

stairs, was the vampire's miasma of swamp gas. Wet slime coated her face and tried to get in her eyes. Horrible smells and even more horrible sounds filled her mouth and ears.

The sounds were shrieks from another world; a dead world; a world of bodies the vampire had already used.

He has been here forever, thought Lacey. He was here before the house, and he will be here after the house. He is evil now, he was evil then, he will be evil after I am gone.

And now, Lacey knew why Bobby was not saying anything. He could not. He was deafened by the screams and the cries and the sobbing of the vampire's past. He was looking right into it.

Bobby *knew*.

The rest of them were just guessing.

But Bobby *knew* what was going to happen to one of them.

Lacey screwed her eyes tightly shut, to keep from seeing the future and the past, and to keep the horrible swamp gas out of her eyes.

Nothing would have made Lacey run down the stairs into that oozing sucking mud.

She pushed harder and harder on Bobby, but nothing happened.

Or at least, nothing happened to Bobby. Lacey herself stumbled back through the door, back into the tower.

Oh! the unbelievable relief of breathing real air again! No smog of corpses, no relics of pain.

On this side of Bobby's pinned figure were four

other normal human beings, with their normal bodies, circulating blood, expanding lungs, functioning brains.

"I know what it is," said Lacey abruptly. She switched off the flashlight.

Sherree screamed. She had a powerful scream, and one which the mansion seemed to appreciate; the scream was welcomed into the terrible dark beyond the door.

Randy whimpered. Zach trembled convulsively. Roxanne's eyes filled with tears.

Lacey said, "I think the dark is better. I think this tower was meant to be dark. I think the flashlight is an invader. We can't use it again."

She was right.

For now that dark had returned, Bobby sank.

Slowly. As if he were at the top of an old playground slide, rusty, no speed to it. A slide for tiny nervous children.

Bobby puddled to the floor of the tower, like Zach in his Halloween memory. Zach and Randy rolled their friend safely back to the center of the room.

In the middle of the tower the six of them huddled.

When Sherree reached out to hold hands, everybody responded.

Then Sherree said, "I can't sit like this. My back is showing. Let's turn around and have all our backs touching, and we'll face out."

"That's worse," said Bobby. His voice had changed. It was dull and leaden. It was not Bobby at all; it was somebody who had known suffering and pain, someone acquainted with fear, someone with no hope.

"Why is it worse?" whispered Sherree. Sherree tried to make herself smaller and smaller, but it was no good; she had spent a lifetime trying to show herself off and she did not know how to go into reverse.

"I've seen what's out there," said Bobby.

Lacey had not seen.

Only heard.

That was enough.

Bobby's voice was like cement. "Don't go out the door," he said. "Nobody go out the door."

Roxanne felt as if the cement were around her feet, and some gangster were going to throw her into the reservoir and drown her.

Bobby read her thoughts. "No," he said, his voice as drowned as the vampire's previous victims. "It's worse than that, Roxanne. Don't go out the door."

Sherree grabbed her boyfriend's shoulders and tried to see his eyes. *"Then how will we get out of here?"* she screamed.

She saw his eyes and wished she had not.

"We won't," said Bobby.

Chapter 4

Lacey's younger brother Kevin, who was in eighth grade, could not believe how long it had taken Lacey to get out of the house. Kevin dimly remembered Lacey telling Mom and Dad she was going to stay at Roxanne's, but apparently she was going to Sherree's instead. Kevin had never heard of either girl and his only interest was being alone in the house at last. Once the house was empty, Kevin had a telephone call to make.

The telephone call.

Kevin was deep in his first real crush.

He had told nobody about the crush, since he had nobody to tell.

His best friend, Will, had made such a complete idiot of himself last spring when Will got a crush on Lauren that Kevin trembled at the mere thought of following in Will's footsteps. Kevin was not going to start by buying a huge silver bracelet for a girl who did not even like to sit near him. He was going to start with a simple phone call.

He was doing his homework, Kevin would say

casually, and he remembered that Mardee . . .

Kevin rehearsed the call over and over. Sometimes his voice sounded triumphantly interesting, and sometimes it sounded as if Kevin were the dwindle-head of the century.

"We're going, dear," said his mother. "Here's the phone number if you have to reach us. We'll be home around one A.M. Be sure to keep the doors locked and don't watch anything disgusting on television."

"Okay, Mom," said Kevin, who always watched disgusting things on television the instant his parents were out the door. The thud of the closing front door and the clack of the closing lock were music to his heart.

He kept the TV on very low volume, for company, and looked up Mardee's number again, although he knew it by memory.

It took him a full hour to manage the actual call. The sixty minutes were filled with half-dialed numbers, self-scolding and swearing, hysterical laughter and deep despair. Kevin knew that if anybody could see him they'd figure he was a maniac. I am a maniac, he thought, I am insane about Mardee. His fingers completed all seven digits this time and to his horror the phone at the other end was actually lifted. "Hello?"

Kevin's tongue felt like a lost mitten. "Hi — Mardee?"

"Yeah?"

"This is Kevin."

"Kevin?"

"From school. Kevin James?"

"Oh, yeah, hi, Kevin, how are you?"

"Fine." His voice was not fine. His hands were sweating so badly they had soaked right through his jeans where they pressed down. Disgusting. What girl wanted to hold hands with a water faucet?

"It's funny you should call," said Mardee. "I was just thinking about you."

"You were?" Kevin was absolutely thrilled.

"My older brother Bobby is at a party with your sister Lacey tonight."

Kevin was puzzled. "Can't be. Lacey's over at Sherree's."

"That's the story," said Mardee. "But you didn't believe it, did you?"

Kevin had always believed every single thing his big sister said. Lacey was the most straightforward and uninteresting person in America.

"Weren't you suspicious when it was Sherree's house they were supposed to be going to?" Mardee was laughing.

Kevin did not know Sherree. How was he supposed to be suspicious?

"Sherree is all body and no mind," said Mardee.

Kevin was pretty sure he would remember meeting somebody like that.

"They're actually going to party all night in the dark in a deserted house," said Mardee.

Kevin was overwhelmed. His sister? Party? "No," said Kevin. "I don't think Lacey parties. She's kind of a — " But Kevin loved Lacey, so he did not say that she was kind of a dwindle-head. But it was true.

"It's a party, all right," said Mardee cheerfully. "Bobby doesn't do anything on Saturday nights but party."

Kevin was rather proud of his sister. It was time she broke forth and did something other than study, practice, work out, and be kind to the elderly. Lacey at a party. Kevin could not quite picture this. He wondered if the others would give her partying lessons.

He wondered what Mardee would be like at a party. Kevin had not done a whole lot of partying in his life, either. Starting with Mardee would be a pleasant introduction. He said, "Mardee."

"Yup. That's my name, don't wear it out."

Kevin had thought they stopped saying that in third grade, but evidently not. He went on manfully. "Mardee, what do you say we — um — " but unfortunately, he was too rattled to remember what he had planned to suggest. The only activity that sprang to mind, he could not suggest aloud on a telephone.

"Yes!" said Mardee.

Kevin was awestruck. Would it be as easy as this?

"I know the address," said Mardee. "Of course, neither one of us has a car, but that could be the fun part."

Kevin was eager to have the fun part.

"It's probably a mile if you walk over to my house," said Mardee, "and probably another mile to the Mall House."

The Mall House? That horrible termite-infested

porch-rotting monstrosity waiting to be ripped down? Kevin was horrified. Of all the places he did not want to go on a first date —

"What we could do is," said Mardee, giggling wildly, "we could scare them. That's why they went there, you know. To be scared. We could add the extras. The special touches. The really good noises. Tapping on window panes. Howling like the wind."

"Let me get this straight. You want me to walk over to your house, get you, we'd walk to that abandoned mansion, creep up in the dark, throw pebbles at the window, hide behind those old fallen trees, and listen to my sister and your brother scream in the dark."

"Right!" cried Mardee. "Won't it be fun?"

Kevin ceased to be an eighth-grade boy striving for adulthood and sex. He became a fifth-grader, dying for Halloween and fake blood, free candy and screaming girls. "I'm on my way," said Kevin. "Find a flashlight."

"A flashlight!" said Mardee, disgusted. "And let them see us? Nosirree. We're going in the pitch dark, buddy."

"Pitch dark," repeated Kevin reverently. All sorts of possibilities sprouted in his beginner mind.

Roxanne held onto the hammer.

If the vampire came near her, she would let him have it. Roxanne was good at sports although she had not gone out for any since Middle School. The coaches were always after her to be on a team, but Roxanne disliked losing anything publicly. It wasn't

so bad to goof up in gym class and it wasn't so bad
to screw up on an exam in an academic class. But
in a gymnasium when the bleachers were filled? On
a playing field when parents and friends lined the
grass?

No, Roxanne liked to stack things in her favor.
And in sports, the odds of being an idiot or doing
poorly were too uncomfortable.

She hefted the hammer. It felt good and strong
in her hand.

"Okay, I'm sorry," said Randy from his corner.
He sounded belligerent, the way people do when
the whole thing is their own fault, when there's
absolutely no way to pin it on anybody else.

Nobody responded.

"I mean, how was I supposed to know?" said
Randy.

Whiner, thought Roxanne. Who needs him? She
concentrated on the shape of the house. So they
could not exit by the door. There had to be another
way out then. She and her hammer would get out.

Years and years ago, the house must have been
handsome. Big and square, wrapped with an immense porch, its wood trim was curlicued, its many
roofs covered with slate, and its beautiful tower had
once risen above the gleaming house like a ship
sailing at sea.

The hedge must once have been delicately green,
enclosing flowers of great beauty and intoxicating
scent.

But the hedge had grown to gargantuan propor-
tions, threatening neighbors and roads. As the

ground around the mansion had been flattened to get ready for building the mall, chain saws had taken those frightening black and green trees down, and bulldozers had heaped them like dead bodies waiting burial.

The six teenagers had skulked around the downstairs with the flashlight. Anything nice had been pried away and carried off: the mantels over the fireplaces were gone, leaving horrible gaping holes around the brickwork. The beautiful woodwork in the study had been taken, exposing the framework of the house, and the mouse nests. In a butler's pantry, there had once been fine cabinets with beveled glass doors. Long gone. Nothing left but the holes where the screws had attached the cabinets to the studs.

The house was pathetic.

They had gone quickly to the second floor, a dangerous expedition, because the beautiful carved banisters had been removed. There was nothing to hold onto.

"At least they left the treads," Bobby had said.

"Unless those are just shadows," Roxanne had added.

Sherree had screamed happily. Sherree was a good screamer, which would be a useful asset as the night continued.

But on the second floor a strange thing had happened.

Nobody could be bothered looking into the empty bedrooms or trying out the damaged window seat.

Another, steeper, set of stairs coaxed them up again.

Roxanne had actually felt drawn, in a sort of reverse gravity.

The railing was still on this stair, and when her hand touched the surface, it felt warm to her. It quivered slightly, as if wired. They had found themselves getting in line to go up, waiting impatiently, staring with fascination at the lifting feet of the kids ahead of them, and then setting their own feet neatly in the spaces just vacated.

It had been a strange breathless parade.

Randy had gone first. It was his hand that closed on the knob of the single door at the top of the stairs. His hand that swung the door out. His foot that crossed the threshold into the tower.

The tower was very high, Roxanne knew.

Although the house was in a valley, the tower was visible from far away. During Roxanne's lifetime, various owners had either kept the shutters tightly closed over the tower's many windows, or entirely opened. With shutters closed, the tower looked angry, like a weapon poised. With shutters open, the tower seemed hungry, its flaps checking the air for food.

Once up in the tower, the six made a strange discovery. Not only did the tower have shutters on the outside, it had them on the inside. The inner shutters were tightly closed, giving the room a strange inside-out look.

Roxanne's hands memorized the hammer. Three

textures: handle, slipcovered in corrugated rubber for a better grip; shaft, smooth cold metal; head, balled and strong with sweeping claws.

This tower — how many feet above the ground was it? Too many to jump, that was for sure.

Randy was still busy apologizing. He sounded like a Boy Scout worried that he might get a demerit.

"Somebody has to rescue us!" said Sherree hysterically.

Lacey considered the possibility of rescue. She thought of the Land Rover, parked so invisibly in the sheltering maze of fallen hemlocks. Nobody would see it. She thought of the careful excuses made to trusting parents. Nobody would worry. There would be no rescue.

"Telephone somebody, Randy!" cried Sherree. "You have a car phone."

Why, Roxanne asked herself, if you had to be imprisoned with somebody, must it be a brainless, selfish goop like Sherree? "The car phone," Roxanne pointed out, "is in the car."

"I didn't think of bringing it in the house," said Randy. "I'm sorry, okay? I mean, I didn't know this was going to happen; okay? I mean, you can't get mad at *me* over this. How was I supposed to know?"

"Keep whining," said Zach. "Because you're right. Tonight you won't win any points in your popularity collection game, Randy. The minute we get out of this, we're never looking at you again."

"We're not getting out of it," said Bobby.

Zach glared at him. "You sure gave up easily.

Get a grip on yourself, Bobby. We need to talk about what we know about vampires. What exactly do they do? What exactly will happen to us if he gets us?"

"I don't want to talk about that!" wailed Sherree.

"If we gather enough knowledge," said Zachary, "we'll know the vampire's weaknesses."

Sherree burst into tears. "I don't want to know anything about vampires! I want to go home!"

Nobody said anything to that. They all wanted to go home.

"I like my life," added Sherree.

They all liked their lives.

"We're wasting time," said Zach. "List the vampire's weaknesses."

Bobby laughed.

Lacey said softly, "The vampire's weaknesses don't count. Our own weaknesses are the ones that matter."

Chapter 5

It was a new sound.

A completely different sound. Almost gentle. A tribal sound, like something from a film on ancient Africa, of hollow logs or old drums.

Lacey had heard the sound before, just as she had smelled the smell before, and seen the cloak before.

I have had other lives, thought Lacey. Were they terrible? Was I as afraid during those lives as I am now? Was I glad to pass into other worlds? Did I go with as much pain and fear as I will this time?

The gentle thrumming continued.

It was precise and rhythmic. It reminded Lacey of somebody absently plucking the bass string on a guitar.

It was a waiting sound: background music: rhythm before the action begins.

Sherree laughed hysterically. "It's the vampire!" she said. "He's knocking." Sherree turned to open the door. "Come in, come in," she sang, like a lost opera soprano. Or a young girl losing her mind.

Only some of the vampire came in. Cloak, rather than teeth. Stench, rather than hands.

Lacey bit her lips, which made her think of teeth, and other, future, bites, and she put both hands over her mouth and shuddered behind the wall of her locked fingers.

"Have you made any progress?" said the vampire courteously.

Lacey hated him for being gentlemanly. This was not a mannerly occasion. She found her voice. "We'll let you know," she said icily, in the rudest voice she could manage.

"You must feel free to take your time," said the vampire. "I have all night, of course."

The cloak evaporated more quickly than before, but his smell was greater and stayed longer. Roxanne had a coughing fit.

"That's it!" whispered Zach, wildly excited. "We'll stall. We'll bluff. We'll waste time!" Zach choked in his eagerness to explain the strategy to the rest. "When the sun comes up, he's out of the picture! I saw that in a movie! Vampires can't live in the sun!"

But the vampire's voice was still among them. He straightened Zach out. "I can make the night last as long as I wish, you see. You chose a sealed house, my friends. Plywood . . . nailed over broken panes. Light sockets . . . without bulbs. Wiring . . . in which no electricity flows. It is always night in this house."

His voice went on shivering for some time.
Always night.

Always night.
Always night.

A shutter caught Zach's attention. It rattled its louvers as if it were talking to him. Zach nearly answered. Then he stopped himself. Those were strips of wood. Nothing else.

I've got to get out of here, he thought. Before I lose my mind.

It seemed to grow darker in the tower. The room added shadows and layers. The walls became farther away, the ceiling more distant.

I have to do something, thought Zach, before we are in total dark and total silence.

Somehow he knew that once the horror became complete, nobody would be able to think, nobody would be able to act, nobody would be able to escape.

His mind tumbled like clothes in a dryer, falling, mindless, knowing nothing but heat and gravity. He could not grip any of his thoughts; he could come to no conclusions; he could plan no strategy.

All night. Their lives would last all night. Their lives would be nothing but night. Endless night.

Unless Zach could find a way out.

"We have to get out of here!" cried Roxanne. "Now! We can't just stand here and pretend somebody is going to rescue us. Nobody is going to rescue us! Somebody do something!"

Roxanne clung to the hammer.

What would happen to the vampire if she swung the hammer at it? Was there anything to bruise or break? Did it have substance or was it some sort of reflection of itself? Did it need — Roxanne could not bear imagining this part — did it need a meal in order to have flesh and skin?

In her panic, Roxanne pressed down with the hammer. It caught in the crack of the floorboards. Her body was so clenched with fear that she was gripped by an involuntary spasm, and she wrenched the hammer upward. The floorboard under which the claws were hooked came upward a half inch.

What's under there? she thought. Roxanne did not know what houses were made of. Beneath this floor would be the ceiling of the room below. What was the room below? What were ceilings made of? What would be in the sandwich of top floor and bottom ceiling? For a moment, she worried about live wires that could electrocute her should she stab a hammer claw through one. Then she remembered the electricity was off. She actually blushed in the dark, grateful that people like Zach, who were intelligent, did not know what a stupid worry she had just entertained.

Roxanne looked down. It was much too dark to see anything. She held tightly to the hammer handle. She pulled harder. The strip of flooring came up another inch. Nothing, absolutely nothing, would have made Roxanne stick bare fingers under the floor. With everything else there was to be afraid of, how did she have energy left to be afraid of touching the open edge of a piece of wood? You would think I'd have reached a fear saturation point, she thought.

But no.

Perhaps you could always become more afraid.

After several moments of gathering courage, Roxanne worked the claws of the hammer a few inches down the flooring strip, and pried again.

Zach touched the shutter. It felt punky. Rotted. Like a piece of tree fallen years ago in a storm, full of insects and becoming mulch on the forest floor. It contained its own damp. It felt as if he could roll it up in his hand.

Instead, he opened the shutter.

At first, although he knew he was looking at sky now, instead of tower wall, he could see no difference. It was nighttime. There was no moon. There were no stars. No plane sparkled red and white in the sky. No immense beam from a car dealership or a carnival circled in the sky.

Zach touched the glass window.

Slowly, he lifted it. It held, staying up.

He put his hand outside into the night air. The vampire might possess the door, but he did not possess this window! Zach said nothing to the others. Who knew what the vampire could feel happening in his own house? Who knew what the vampire saw? Best not to start loud frantic conversations on the subject of getting out via the window.

Zach thrust his head and shoulders through the opening.

The air was fresh and clear.

He had not realized the extent of the vampire's pollution until his face was breathing in clean air. The vampire had so completely contaminated the tower they might have been breathing exhausts of decrepit trucks.

Over and over again Zach filled his lungs with the wonderful clean oxygen of the night sky.

There was no longer really a yard around the old mansion. There were ditches and troughs where bulldozers had gouged away shrubs, or stone garden paths. The bulldozers had not followed up on their task. Heaped around the ground were little dirt and debris mountains. If Kevin had been a little boy, and had had his toy trucks along, he would have had a wonderful time road-building.

"There's the car,"whispered Mardee. "They're here, all right."

Randy's Land Rover was a dark color and blended into the fallen hemlocks like a jungle animal into dense leaves. Kevin had not even seen it. There was something terrifying about the way it was parked. Randy must have driven into the Mall House yard, circled, and backed carefully into the immense black branches, with their evil stubs of broken limbs stabbing the air all around them. Somebody had had to get out of the Land Rover first and direct him, or they would have been stabbed onto the prongs of the dead trees like meat on a fork.

The house was sordid and ruined.

There was nothing romantic about it.

It had a caved-in look, a place so completely gone, so completely lost, that even homeless drug addicts and mentally ill street people would not come here. The building itself looked mentally ill, its shutters crooked, its shingles curled upward, its roofing sagged.

The silence around the mansion was complete.

Life had stopped here. No birds, no small animals, perhaps not even any insects. No heart beat here. No lungs filled.

Life had stopped here. No flowers, no shrubs, no trees, perhaps not even weeds or grass. No roots dug into the fruitful earth. No leaves drew sustenance from the heavy air.

The air was truly heavy, as if the weather were about to change. Or as if something evil and unthinkable were passing through.

Kevin and Mardee found that they were holding not hands, but bodies. As if, should they stand apart, something else would fill that little space between them, and separate them forever.

On the lower floor, sheets of plywood had been nailed over the windows. The pale plywood made blind eyes against the dark house walls.

"They can't be in there," whispered Kevin. "There's no way in."

"They got in somehow; their car's here," breathed Mardee. "Let's go around the house and see how they broke in."

Kevin did not want to circle that house. He did not want to be near that house, or see that house, or even smell that house. Kevin was not actually gagging, but the smell of the house filled him and became part of him, and he felt weirdly older. As if that smell were carrying his body through its lifespan, and by dawn he would be ancient, used up, ready for burial.

Kevin wet his lips and regretted it. The smell gathered substance and landed on his damp lips, coating them. He tried to rub it off on his sleeve. It didn't come off.

Mardee was hanging onto him with both hands now. Kevin tried to enjoy this, but enjoying anything was impossible under the circumstances. Kevin could not imagine his fastidious, careful sister actually going inside.

Lacey wants to be popular, thought Kevin. I guess we all do. Her new friends were going in this horrible place, so she took a deep breath and went along.

Though how anybody could take a deep breath around this house, Kevin could not imagine. Earth and air percolated a vile stench. It was too dark to see the ground.

The source of the smell must be lying open — a septic pit — a sewer tank — a poison disposal field. Kevin put one foot ahead of the other knowing he had never done anything so stupid, but doing it anyway. They circled the house, and found nothing to show where the others had gotten in.

"Maybe they didn't get in," muttered Kevin. "Maybe they fell into whatever pit it is we keep smelling."

Mardee shook her head. Her hair brushed his cheek and briefly he forgot the house and turned his face down into her hair, intoxicated by it. It was satin compared to his own. His was like the tips of old paintbrushes; hers was like ribbons. In the deep darkness he could see into her eyes, the only bright spots on the earth. Kevin forgot the cesspits he had worried about and fell into Mardee's eyes instead.

Mardee whispered, "Let's go up on the porch and see if we can peel back any of the plywood."

Girls were supposed to be so romantic. How come he had to choose one who concentrated on things like this?

I'm wasting time, Zachary thought.

Zach came from a family in which time was never wasted. It was important to make the best possible use of all time. Zach's mother had had an extensive program of cultural activities for Zach when he was young; they had always been going to the Egyptian wing of the museum, or the children's concert and lecture at the symphony. Zach's father set an example of always having a book along to read should they be caught in traffic or have to sit an extra half hour in a doctor's waiting room. Zach's parents saw to it that all summer vacations were Important Experiences and all evening events were Meaningful and Packed with Knowledge.

Zach counted his breaths, and when he had taken ten lung-restoring heaves, he knew that was sufficient and he had no right to waste time tasting air, when he could be thinking up an escape.

By now his eyes were used to the dark and that made Zach feel better; time had not been wasted; he had just been acclimating himself to the dark.

He was three very high stories up in the air. If he were to jump, he would certainly break a leg. If not a spine. Zach had no desire to be a paraplegic. On the other hand, he had no desire to be a vampire's long-awaited dinner.

"Actually," Lacey was saying, in her methodical way, "we wouldn't be his dinner. The correct meaning of breakfast is to break the fast, and the vampire has been fasting for a long time now. So we'd be breakfast."

"Thank you for clearing that up," said Roxanne sarcastically.

Zach actually grinned. Then he studied the roof. There was a sort of gutter around the base of the tower. If he could wriggle out, he could perhaps use that as a crawl space, and inch his way to the roof beam of the rest of the house, which was of course lower than the tower. Perhaps he could slither along the roof beam and find his way down to the roof over the big porch. Then when he dropped to the ground he'd have a much better chance of living through it.

But what if the gutter were as rotten as the shutters? He'd still fall.

Zach was not a physical daredevil.

That was Bobby's style.

Zach preferred to let others take the risks, while he got the excellent grades, made the brilliant jokes, and led the pack.

But he did not see any way out of this except physical daring.

The thought was exhilarating. Zach had been brought up to conquer the world. This was his moment. Yes. It was time. Now he had to take the world by the shoulders and show it what he could do.

Once I'm down, thought Zach, I'll find the nearest telephone and get the fire department over here. They have the high ladders. They'll get the rest out.

Zach knew that he would not call the fire department. He could not dial 911 and tell them to rescue his friends from a vampire. It was too ridiculous. Nobody would believe him. He would be laughed at. Zach could take anything except being laughed at. People would point at him, and chuckle, and call him names. *That's the kid who thought there was a vampire in that old shack they're tearing down to build a mall, isn't that hysterical?*

The tower's exterior shutters banged eagerly, a drumroll for whatever happened next.

His right leg felt the air. His hands gripped the sill tightly. He tried not to think of the great distance to the hard, hard earth. He managed to press his knee against the steeply sloping slates and drag the other leg out.

Good thing I'm not a big guy, thought Zach, who had always before wanted to be a big guy.

His shoes tried to find the gutter he had seen from the window.

But all they found was slick roof, and more slick roof.

His fingers began to ache. He could not grip the sill much longer. He had to put some of his weight on his feet instead of his hands. He kicked, trying to find a footrest.

Something touched his right hand.

Something foul and wet, like a moldy leftover in the refrigerator. He hung on only because his life was in the balance. He could not see what touched his hands. After a few seconds, it did not simply touch his fingers. It applied pressure.

Something was peeling his fingers off the sill.

Somebody had decided to help him fall.

Zach began to scream. He tried to shift his finger grip, but the sill was slick.

He began to fall.

I'm going to die, thought Zach, quite clearly.

He tried to dig his fingernails into the punky wood. He tried to haul himself back into the tower. He screamed for the others to grab him, but nobody came.

With a satisfied little chuckle, the creature peeling him away finished its task, and it leaned forward to watch Zach's fall.

The last thing he saw was a face neither white nor black, skin neither tanned nor pale — but absolutely clear. A face that went right through to the other side, all its interior on display, like some horrible living laboratory model.

And then he was airborne, and screaming his last scream.

Chapter 6

Mardee's scream could have pulled the rest of the nails out of the plywood.

Kevin could not let go of the wood he had hauled back, or it would snap against her and stab her to the window frame. Mardee was still standing next to him and yet she seemed to be pulled forward, into the house.

Something was pulling her by the hair.

Like taffy, Mardee stretched. Her scream went on and on, as if it, too, were being pulled out of her throat, taut like a rubber band.

Kevin put all his strength into the plywood and actually tore it the rest of the way off the house. He flung it down onto the porch floor. He grabbed Mardee and yanked her back against himself. She did not come easily. She felt as if she had been stuck with adhesive. He whipped her around to face him.

The scream stopped. Mardee's face, whiter than any moon or star, was twisted in such horror that Kevin could only imagine she had looked into the scene of a terrible mass murder.

"What happened?" he whispered. His heart was racing, double-timing, working so hard he felt crazed with its speed.

Mardee was as close to him as another skin. "Didn't you feel it, Kevin?" she whispered. She wet her lips, gasping for breath. "Didn't you see it?"

"See what?" He had been busy prying the plywood back from the window. He had not seen much except wood. Why were they whispering? What was happening? What had —

"A vampire," said Mardee.

He was technically rather young, the car thief.

He had dropped out of school before he was sixteen, and spent time in prison before he was twenty, and that had aged him. He was older and more cruel than his actual years.

There was nothing nice about him. He did not have a heart of gold, he did not feel neighborly love. He did not mind injuring people who got in his way. People often got in his way, and he often injured them. He never thought about them when he hurt them and he never thought about them afterward. He did not have a conscience.

What he mostly had was a great need for money.

It had been a difficult summer. Things kept going wrong. In spite of the people he had hurt, the car thief had not acquired any cash.

He had no particular destination in mind as he roamed the streets. He had no particular plan in mind. All he had in mind was greed.

He was panting with it.

He could think only of money and what he would do with it; what he .would buy with it; how much better life would be once he had some.

He did not normally walk down the valley road. Of course, he did not normally walk anywhere, but he had lost his various forms of transportation, and so he was reduced to this pathetic, loser style of going someplace.

He had to walk.

It outraged him that he was on foot. People like him did not deserve this humiliation. Somebody would pay for this, he would see to that.

The car thief walked onto the site where the shopping mall would soon begin to rise. In the dark, it was a shambles. Piles of dirt and trash. Ruts from immense tires. Metal barrels, old railroad ties, and discarded junk. A few scattered, white-painted barriers making a feeble attempt to close off a huge area.

He crossed the acreage hoping to find something — anything — that he could steal and sell. Perhaps a backhoe worth tens of thousands of dollars that he could somehow start up, drive off in the night.

There was nothing.

He walked toward a huge shapeless stack. It had no shadows because there was no light to cast them. It was not until he was very, very close that he realized the stack had no theft potential; it was a bunch of huge old dead trees bulldozed down and left to rot.

He was furious.

He kicked a tree.

But it was not satisfying to kick a tree. It didn't whimper, or cry out, try to run, or hand over its wallet. He wanted a human to kick. Something where you could laugh when it cried out.

He kicked the tree again, and felt no better that time, either.

But he saw something.

Something . . . something large . . . glittered faintly within the trees.

He began to work his way around the branches to get at the thing within them.

It was, thought Roxanne, a vampire without its cloak.

A vampire without its skin.

Nothing but the interior: the silhouette of its bones and its organs.

It seemed to come out from between the shutters, first as flat as a pane of glass, and then thickening, and becoming more visible. It was grinning, its teeth exposed like a dentist's drawing. It peeled Zach off the windowsill and grinned even more widely as Zach screamed and fell.

Zach's screams came from everywhere.

Then they ceased.

He could not have lived.

Well, thought Roxanne, that's one way to escape being the vampire's victim. Die first. Poor Zach. Poor, poor Zach! He had so many plans.

Roxanne found that she was weeping. Her face was covered with tears for Zach. Or was it for herself?

How selfish am I? thought Roxanne. I will know tonight. We will all know tonight.

She thought of the vampire's requirement. Oh, it was truly evil! Not only did they have to witness the "event" — they would have to participate in it; they would have to choose, and live with that choice.

She found that while Zach was falling, and her eyes were weeping, her hand and her hammer had continued prying up floorboards.

"What are you doing?" hissed Randy, hearing the creaks and snaps.

Roxanne shook her head, but of course he couldn't see her. She had managed to lift a whole length of board and now she shifted her hammer to start on the adjacent strip of wood.

She had no idea what she was doing, or why. Perhaps since they could not go out the windows, and they could not go out the door, they would just descend right through the floor.

"What are you doing?" hissed Randy again. Louder.

Randy's such a stupid person, thought Roxanne. The vampire hadn't noticed yet. Roxanne certainly didn't want him to notice *her* now — let alone the possible escape route she was uncovering.

Ten miles away, in an isolated subdivision of only nine houses, a mother and father were furious because their sixteen-year-old son had not brought the family car home. "He was told to be here now, or else!" said the father.

"Now, Dad," said their other child. She was eighteen, and sympathetic to lateness. "He'll be home in a minute. Don't panic."

"I am not panicking, Ginny. I am furious. Your brother is dead."

"No, he's not," said Ginny reassuringly. "He's fine."

"I don't mean he's lying dead in a road somewhere," shouted the father. "I mean, I'm gonna kill him! I told him to get that car home by nine or die. So he's dead." The father stormed back and forth in the tiny front hall. "I should never have let him get his driver's license. I'm taking it away the minute he walks in the door. He's dead."

"Now, Dad," said Ginny. "You and Mom haven't missed much of the party. The Kramers will party till dawn, you know that. If you don't get there for another few minutes, it won't be the end of the world."

"It'll be the end of your brother's world," said the father. "He was told he could take the car for the first half of the evening but we had to have it for the second half. If he ruins our weekend, I'm ruining his *year*."

Ginny thought she saw a way to get something good out of this situation. "The moral of the story," she said cheerfully, "is that our family should have a second car." She smiled hopefully.

Her parents gave her a tight-lipped glare.

Oh, well, thought Ginny. Worth a try.

Out in the driveway a car appeared. But it was not her missing brother. It was Ginny's date. "Jordan and I could drop you at your party, if you want, Dad."

Her father refused to be mollified. "Your mother and I will wait, thank you, until your worthless brother gets here."

Her date bounded up the door. Jordan was one of these courteous-to-adults types, who wanted to hear the whole story. "Are you worried about your son's safety?" asked Jordan, getting deeply concerned and worried himself.

"The time to worry about my brother's safety," said Ginny dryly, "will be when he arrives home."

"Yes, of course we're worried!" said Ginny's mother. "This just is not like him! He's a very responsible boy!"

Ginny rolled her eyes. There was no such thing as a very responsible boy.

Jordan said, "Hey, no probleem-oh. Ginny and I will cruise around and find him."

Ginny, who had been looking forward to something else entirely, was quite irritated. "Really," she said, "I'm sure he's fine. He'll be here in a minute."

"I'd like that, Jordan," said Ginny's mother. "I am genuinely worried. He knows what his father would do to him if he's late tonight. He knows how important it is. So why isn't he here? Anything could have happened! He could have had an accident! He could be bleeding somewhere!" Ginny's mother had worked herself up into tears. "He could have been stolen away! We'll never see him again."

Ginny tried to bring a little reality to the situation. "Mom. He's six-two. He lifts weights. He could bench press a station wagon. Nobody stole him away. We're going to see him again. Probably in five minutes."

But Ginny's date loved this kind of thing. He loved action and heroism. Jordan would much rather cruise the entire city and all its suburbs, tracking down a lost child, than go to a party where somebody had rented a movie he had probably already seen, and then order pizza, which, after all, he had just eaten for lunch. The fact that the lost child was bigger and stronger than Jordan was did not matter.

"We'll find him," Jordan promised. "Don't worry! We'll look everywhere!" He took Ginny's hand and bounded with her back to the car. Full of enthusiasm, he switched on the engine, revved the motor, crammed the gear stick into first, and left a patch on the street. "Where do we start?" he said happily. He was already looking left and right, peering behind shrubs and picket fences.

Ginny regarded him stonily. Then she turned on the radio, put the volume where she liked it, and said, "Somebody's having a party at that horrible old mansion. The Mall House. Maybe he decided to crash that."

Her date sighed with pleasure.

He did not come to a full stop at the end of the little housing division road. He looked swiftly both ways, and instead accelerated through the stop sign and let his tires scream as he turned left.

Ginny sighed. It was going to be a long night.

And all for a brother.

When you got right down to it — who needed him?

Lacey could not stop hearing the scream.

Even though she knew that Zach must have hit the ground by now, must be crushed flat against it, she could still hear the scream.

Zach! she thought numbly.

Bobby and Zach were the kind of boys to whom nothing bad ever happened; they were inoculated against trouble from birth. Their lives went smoothly, their complexions went smoothly, their relationships went smoothly.

And now look. Zach was dead or broken. Bobby was catatonic.

In the silence of the tower room, into the muffled panting and weeping of the five left standing there, came a new sound.

A rhythmic series of thuds.

Steps coming up the stairs.

Lacey's heart roared like a locomotive.

The vampire had not made noise before. Whose step was so heavy? Perhaps a real person was walking up those stairs.

Could it be the police, coming to see what was going on? To find out who had screamed? Were they about to be rescued?

Was it some horrible drug-crazed murderer escaped from an insane asylum?

Lacey could not bear to look at the door, but neither could she look away. It was as though her eyes no longer belonged to her, but were ruled by some other force.

Be the police! she thought, and prayed, and begged. Please be the police. Please save us! Please end this! We don't deserve this! We want to go home! We want our mothers! We —

Through the door came the vampire.

His cloak swirled and his stench rose up.

Under his arm was the burden that gave him weight.

Zach's body.

Chapter 7

"A vampire?" repeated Kevin James. He actually began to laugh.

"Don't you laugh at me," snapped Mardee.

"I can't help it. A *vampire?*"

Mardee pulled back from him. The creep. To think that she was alone with this idiot. Nothing, nothing in the entire world, was more maddening than somebody who laughed at you. Mardee pulled her lips together in a furious pout. She folded her arms over her chest. "Yes," she said. "A vampire."

Kevin laughed again, and louder.

It was a Land Rover.

The car thief grinned widely. Some of his teeth had rotted, and some were missing.

Somebody had already stolen the Land Rover once, obviously, or it wouldn't be here. Some fool who had not had the foresight to drive it out of state, or provide a closed garage. Some beginner who had tucked it here until morning.

Well, come morning, it would not be here.

68

Land Rovers. That whole class of vehicles made the car thief laugh. Big, high, tough Jeeps, bought exclusively by weak and wimpy suburbanites. Big strong Jeeps for difficult terrain and steep grades, that would never go anywhere except a parking lot.

And loaded. These babies always had a great sound system. Air conditioning. Telephones. Last summer he even got one that had a fax machine in it.

The car thief felt around the cracks of the doors. In the complete dark it would not be easy to break in.

He did not think he had ever been anywhere as dark as this.

Although he was rarely afraid — he preferred to scare others than to be scared — the car thief felt a prickle on the back of his neck.

It was not fear. It was not some sixth sense.

It was an actual touch.

Fingers brushed his neck.

The car thief bit back a scream and whirled, ready to strike back.

Nothing was there.

He was left trembling, his knees jellied.

He hated that. It made him deeply angry that anything could frighten him.

Nothing was there, he told himself. And yet that outraged him. He did not make things up! He did not get scared of the dark!

His hands went back to feeling around the door. His hands were trembling and sweaty. He ground his teeth together, to get rid of the debilitating fear.

And again, gently, exploring, lifting the long hair that lay against the neck of his T-shirt, came the touch. Something was actually feeling the back of his neck, exactly imitating the way he was feeling the car.

He whipped around for a second time, and this time he struck blindly into the air, making fists, fighting it.

But nothing was there.

It must have been the tip of a branch. A wavering end of one of these dead trees. It had, actually, felt dead. Even though it had moved, touching him.

The car thief ran his bare hands through the air, as one feeling for a spiderweb. But he encountered no branch, no web, that could have touched the back of his neck.

Instead there came a new sensation. A smell. A smell like raw sewage. It rose up around his ankles as if he were sinking into some terrible hole.

He grabbed at the only thing available. The door handle of the Land Rover. He gripped that faint silvery shine.

And the door opened.

The Land Rover was not locked. .

The car thief grinned.

"Let's go get some ice cream," said Kevin. The entire evening was so weird. He kept laughing. Who would ever have thought you could have a first date like this? Who could he even tell about this?

"Your sister is in there with a vampire and you

want to have ice cream?" said Mardee. She was outraged.

"If my sister were in there," Kevin pointed out, "she would have said something by now. She had to have heard your scream."

Mardee looked at him in astonishment. "I didn't scream," she said.

The vampire carried Zach like a grocery bag. Set him on the floor like a loaf of bread.

Mildly he said to the others, "This is wasting time, you know. Not that I didn't appreciate the effort, dear boy," he added. "It was most interesting. And the scream — quite well done. I like a good scream." The vampire reflected on this. "In fact," he said, "I am a connoisseur of screams."

"In that case," said Lacey, "you will get absolutely nothing from us but silence, you dirtbag."

"Lacey!" hissed Randy. "Don't call him names. It'll make him angry."

Lacey stared at Randy incredulously. What possible difference could it make if the vampire was angry? His teeth were just as sharp.

In the mournful voice of a school principal yearning to retire, the vampire explained that they had disregarded his directions. It really was time for them to begin their important decision.

"Buzz off," said Lacey. "Are you all right, Zach?"

Zach sat up and brushed himself off. The tower room was quite light. The vampire was giving off the phosphorescence again. Zach looked around in a daze. He looked down at his fingers, which had been peeled away from the sill, and his legs, which had not been broken against the ground below.

"You caught me," he said to the vampire. "You saved my life."

The vampire said sympathetically, "You had an assignment to complete, as you recall. This is not homework. You may not skip it and average your grade. Tonight you will choose."

Zach closed his eyes. He had not closed his eyes when he was falling. But the knowledge that he had accomplished nothing, that he was still here, that he still faced one chance in six — it was too much to look at. So he closed his eyes. With his eyes still closed he said, "If you were going to save me, why did you peel my fingers away from the sill to start with?"

The vampire was insulted. "I would never do a thing like that," he said.

"Then who did?" said Zach.

"I don't suppose anybody did," said the vampire. "How would it have benefited your companions to do that? The sill was slick and you had a poor grip, that's all. It was a poor plan to start with."

Roxanne stared at the vampire. She had seen him. With her very own eyes. She had watched him send Zach plunging to the ground.

"Let us return to the primary consideration," said the vampire.

"No," said Lacey. "Dry up and blow away." She glared fiercely, as if she actually expected this third-grade curse to accomplish something. The vampire merely looked at her with more interest than he looked at the others, so Lacey quickly looked away again. She happened to look toward Randy.

Poor Randy was losing his grip. Perhaps it was because he was the only boy who had not yet attempted escape. Perhaps he felt a manly duty to hurl himself in some outward direction, but there were none left.

Randy was pulling things out of his pockets and fondling them like lucky charms. He had his keys in one hand; he had a Bic pen, which he continuously capped and uncapped; he had a disposable lighter, whose slick plastic side he stroked with his thumb; he had several quarters, which he tumbled from one palm to another.

Bobby seemed marginally more aware than he had been, but he still wore a fogged and stunned look.

Sherree was sitting in a little ball, hugging her knees to her chest, rocking back and forth.

Roxanne appeared to be trying to scrape through the floor with her fingernails.

Lacey was furious with the vampire. Who was he to do this to them? She whirled back to face him. When Lacey was angry, she screwed up her face so that all her features met in the center, wrinkled and sharp. "We do have things to discuss, actually," said Lacey, glaring. "We will begin with your character. Or lack of character. I demand to know why you do terrible things like this to innocent people."

"I don't do anything terrible." He was affronted by the accusation.

"It isn't nice to kill people."

"This is nature," explained the vampire. "Nature is built on the laws of birth and death. Predator and victim. Hawk and mouse."

The six were not happy with that metaphor. Even Bobby in his daze flinched. No one ever wants to be the victim or the mouse.

"But I don't kill anyone, if you need details," said the vampire. "No, you see, after the . . . event . . . we will call it an *event* . . . you will be very tired. There will not be much left of you. Not much personality. Not much energy. Not much for people to bother with. You will become a shadow of your former self."

They cherished their characters. They were proud of their personalities. They liked who they were.

A shadow of that? Not much left? Nothing for other people to bother with?

"Perhaps," said the vampire, his voice like chocolate, dark and slippery, "to hasten the final ending, each of you should present a defense to the others. Each of you should explain to the other five why he or she should — or should not — be the choice."

"That is sick," said Lacey sharply. "We are not going to lower ourselves to your level."

Randy said nervously. "I'm not so sure you're right, Lacey." It seemed to Randy if the vampire had all the facts, he might make the choice himself. That would be so much easier. Randy felt he was carrying enough guilt. It was his fault they were here at all. He did not want to carry more. On the other hand, he did not want to be the choice.

"We are not going to let you have anybody," Lacey informed the vampire. "You may as well face that, you hairball. We didn't come here to be your choice."

The vampire definitely did not like being called names. His snarl seemed to cross the room, independently of his cloak and form. His teeth overlapped, as if he were biting his own chin, and his upper lip twitched like a dog guarding a back door.

Sheeree began to make dog noises herself, whimpering and moaning.

"You came here for adventure," the vampire pointed out to Lacey. "I am giving it to you." His snarl turned into a caricature of a smile. "Never wish for anything," he whispered joyfully. "You might get it!"

"You may leave now," said Lacey imperiously. "And don't come back."

The vampire ignored her. He met the eyes of each of the other five. "One of you will be given to me by the others," he said gently. "And that is that. However long the night, however difficult the choice, you will complete the assignment."

Roxanne had completed every assignment of her life.

Roxanne had been well organized since first grade, and always knew what chapter they were on, and which outline was due on Friday, and which quiz would be given on Monday.

And Roxanne intended to complete the rest of

her life as well. This was her senior year! She had college out there, and a yearbook. A prom, and a future. She couldn't be letting some vampire suck her life away.

The vampire disappeared. He did not seem to go out the door, but simply faded slowly. You could not tell whether he was still in the room or not. Roxanne counted to one hundred before she began prying at the floor again.

Roxanne saw her dreams turn into reflections in a cracked mirror. Roxanne moved on to the third floorboard and yanked.

The house was full of its own noises. Its shutters banged and its roof clattered. Its porches creaked and its shingles curled. Roxanne's noise blended into the fabric of the night. And whatever was below her made no noise of its own. Instead it made a smell. As if the vampire were not enough of a stink, a new one rose from between the floors.

"Shut up!" said Mardee fiercely. She hated Kevin now. She could not believe she had thought spending an evening with a boy would be fun. Boys. Ugh. They were disgusting. They laughed at you. Lives were in danger and what did they do? They suggested ice cream.

Kevin put his hand tightly over his own mouth, making a gag from his palm, pantomiming absolute silence. Behind his palm he grinned insanely. He was really having an excellent time. Weird. But excellent.

The laugh that had so angered Mardee, however, continued.

From out in the yard, and from up in the tower, separate laughs spun through the fetid air.

One laugh was as high-pitched as a broken piccolo.

The other laugh was deep and mucky as oil wells.

Both were evil.

On their heads, the hair shivered. Kevin's hair shifted position as if fingers were going through it; as if the laugh possessed hands to examine his scalp. Mardee's hair blew around as if some tiny private tornado had settled in it.

Kevin was terrified.

It made him furious. Terror was for girls. What was with this panic seizing him?

He wanted to wet his lips but could not bring himself to open his mouth. Something would fly into his mouth if he parted his lips. From behind the protection of his own palm he whispered to Mardee, "Let's go sit in the Land Rover."

Roxanne had six floorboards lifted.

It was like war, fighting the nails, but the way Lacey was riling up the vampire, he was going to quit the original option of choice and just hurl himself on somebody's throat. Roxanne wanted to be gone, and if she had to dig through another layer of horror, so be it.

Needing more leverage, Roxanne stood up.

Ignoring the stares of the others, pulling and

yanking on the boards, she found herself taking immense pride in her strength. Nails snapped free and boards splintered.

The nails screamed as they were ripped out. Or was it the vampire screaming?

Roxanne could not spare the time to look up or look around.

She had the misfortune to be looking down, therefore, when she finished opening up the floor. She had found the vampire's cell.

His sleeping place.

His coffin.

Roxanne fainted, falling directly into the rotting nest she had exposed.

Chapter 8

The vampire was gone.

It was so strange. The fetid atmosphere of the tower was simply air. The overwhelming slimy horror of the place had vanished. The murmuring of the past, those victims whose souls lay under the mansion, ceased.

Lacey walked in a slow circle around the tower room. She touched the walls.

It was just a house.

Plaster.

Glass.

Wood.

Nothing more.

"*He left*," whispered Sherree. She stood up from her crouch and dusted herself off, as if she had been sitting on the sand at the beach and was ready to go in the water now. Immediately Sherree began worrying again what she looked like, and whether her hair still looked good, and if she needed to reapply her lipstick, and if she'd wrecked her clothes from the dust and ickies that floated around this horrible place. She wanted a mirror so she could do a proper inspection of her face. Sherrée dug deep into her pocketbook, searching for her mirror.

Bobby came out of his trance. When he was still pinned in the air, he had been forced to stare into the ruined lives of the humans the vampire had taken over the decades. The horror of their destruction had turned his mind to ice. His screams had tightened in his throat and turned solid, and his heart seemed to thud in a vacuum, keeping him alive, but giving him no warmth, no pulse.

When he had come down, he was a blank.

It was truly like being half dead. Bobby had been able to investigate himself: He had seen that his flesh continued to function in its earthly way, taking in the air it needed, circulating the blood it required. And yet he was not all there. His mind — his soul — his very self — whatever those things were composed of: they hung suspended.

He had thoughts, but they were distant. His thoughts seemed to have traveled out of state. Or out of body. His thoughts floated around him without meaning anything to him.

Bobby, the consummate athlete, had never before had no grip on himself. No possession of his abilities.

But now the vampire was gone. Bobby looked around, confused and disoriented, but himself. He felt his personality come back, as if it lay in puddles around the room, and was now tilting, sliding, coming back into the jar of his mind. I'm me again, he thought. The vampire didn't take me after all. He just showed me what he can do.

Zachary's body had not slowed like Bobby's. While Bobby had seemed to enter a mental hibernation, Zach had entered a horrible trembling: a constant vibration. Even when he could not see his muscles quiver, even when he could not observe his joints shivering, he could feel his corpuscles and cells shuddering. His complete interior, everything under his skin, was shaken by the fall. Shaken by being caught. Shaken by the taste and flavor and stench and feel of the vampire's cloak.

That cloak that had draped itself over his body. Truly it had been the lining from thousands of coffins. It was not moss, yet it was wet and green and growing. Every centimeter of his skin had recoiled in horror at its touch.

The vampire itself had never touched Zach.

He had been caught and picked up and removed to the tower by the cloak. Zach had not even been able to feel the vampire's arms supporting him, although they must have. What strength could a cloak have?

But now the vampire was gone.

The vampire's departure was so complete that Zach's body knew it right down into the depths of his gut, and he ceased to shake from his fall.

The vampire was gone.

Zach was afraid to look around. In his shuddering self-oriented existence, had he missed the "event"? Had the vampire taken a victim while Zach was busy trembling? Was Zach going to count heads and find there were now only five teenagers in the tower? Who would the sixth be? Which of this group was missing now? Missing forever? Missing into that unspeakable horror that had scraped Zach's skin? Peeled Zach's fingers from the window and yet caught him at the bottom?

And where? Where would that sixth one be, right now? Swallowed in that cloak? Feeling the jaws of —

Zach wrenched his mind away, and counted.

He saw Bobby. He saw Lacey. He saw Randy. He saw Sherree. For one long, hideous, ghastly moment, he could not see Roxanne. And then his eyes lit on her: half fallen right through the floor.

Zach's body heaved itself in one last final shudder, more of a convulsion, really, and he stumbled forward to try to get Roxanne out of whatever pit she had slid into.

Their fingers met, and Roxanne's were surprisingly warm and calm.

Roxanne was rather proud of herself. She was actually lying in the dreadful cavity of the vampire's hibernation, and yet she was no longer afraid. For several fine moments she congratulated herself on her courage; awarded herself prizes for being the bravest on earth. Then she realized that the vampire had disappeared. Her own bravery — or lack of it — had nothing to do with the situation. There was no longer anything to be afraid of. The vampire had left.

But where? thought Roxanne. Where does he go

when he's not here? He can't get into this nest. I'm in it. And if he were here, visible or invisible, I would know.

So where is he?

"He's gone!" repeated Sherree cheerfully. Sherree did a little dance. She tapped both toes and heels in a happy pattern on the wooden floor of the tower. She rocked a little, swayed a little, giggled a little. "Let's get a move along, guys! Time to roll. Time to close the curtain on this little show." Sherree headed for the door.

But Lacey frowned. She preferred to have an understanding of events. "What could have made him leave?" said Lacey. She was suspicious. What was going on here?

"Roxanne invaded his nest," said Zach. "I think he had to flee."

Zach, Bobby, Randy, and Lacey stared down into the ghastly little coffinlike space between the floors.

Sherree stomped her feet. "What is with you idiots?" she shouted. "Stop worrying about the vampire's housing situation!"

Lacey and Roxanne giggled in spite of themselves.

Sherree said, "Come on, you guys. The night is still young. We can party some place intelligent instead of this dump."

Roxanne said, "You know, Sherree, I'm starting to like you." Lacey, Roxanne, and Sherree giggled together, not quite sure what was funny, but finding themselves together in some girlish emotion.

Roxanne started to get out.

"Stop!" shouted Randy. He actually pushed her back in.

"What am I supposed to do?" Roxanne shouted right back. "Set up housekeeping? Of course I'm getting out of here. Help me." She stuck out one hand to Randy and Zach took the other.

"Listen to me!" said Randy fiercely. "Zach is right. The vampire left because you invaded his nest. And that means," said Randy, "he'll come back the minute you're out of it."

Roxanne shook Randy's hand free. Then, feeling her oats, she shook Zach's off also. She was very pleased with herself, getting out of the opening with help from nobody. I'm tough, she thought. I'm strong. I'm proud. "You are such a loser, Randy," she said.

Lacey tested the open doorway.

There was nothing in the door space but air.

The vampire no longer possessed the door. Nothing at all possessed the door. It was just a door.

"We can leave," she said briefly. "Come on, everybody. There's no time to waste."

Sherree giggled again, and danced her way over the floor. "Wow, Randy, I mean — like — you told us this would be a night to remember. How did you do it? Did you hire an actor or something?" The vampire had been gone only minutes, and yet he was sliding from Sherree's mind. Already she wondered if this was some weird combination of hologram and costume. Sherree caught Randy's rejected hand and swung it happily. Randy had indeed given them a night to remember. In Sherree's mind, Randy had gained points.

Roxanne discovered that she had physical proof of the vampire's existence. The vampire's leavings clung to her skin. It was as if she'd coated herself with suntan lotion: vampire oil was all over her flesh.

While Lacey, ever cautious, crept toward the tower opening, and Sherree danced, and Randy worried, and Zach and Bobby gathered momentum and courage, Roxanne was forced to look down at her very own body, which had lain in a vampire's nest.

Roxanne came very close to throwing up.

When she got home, Roxanne thought, she would take a shower several hours long. She would use Clorox and Ajax instead of Ivory soap. By the time she was done, it would be daylight and she would dry herself in the yellow sun, soaking up safety and light. She would revel in those precious hours in which vampires could not function.

And if they ever did build that new mall here, on this very site, she, Roxanne, would never shop in it. Because who knew? Who knew where else a vampire could dig in? Who knew what cracks in new buildings his stinking spirit might find?

"Hurry up," said Lacey. Her voice was taut with urgency.

Roxanne moved to the center of the group. Let Sherree and Randy go first. Let the vampire grab their ankles and yank on their hair. Roxanne hung on to Lacey's belt.

The group was going too slowly for Roxanne. She began herding her friends along, as if she were a sheepdog. "Go on, go on," she said, practically nipping them. "We don't have all night!"

Randy and Sherree reached the small landing at the top of the stairs.

Sherree took the first step down.

Nothing happened.

She took a second step.

Roxanne could almost hear six separate hearts whacking chest walls, pumping furiously. Her own heart was going insane with the need to move, to run, to race, to get out of here while there was time! "What are you waiting for?" shouted Roxanne. "Get going!"

Nobody was in the tower now. Three of them were on the stairs, three were crowded onto the little landing.

Don't look back! thought Bobby. Whatever I saw when I was pinned in air, it's back there! I must not look back. I must not look down. I just have to get out! Out! Out!

Bobby caught the nearest hand. It was Lacey's. He had never held anything so gratefully.

Bobby would have shoved the rest forward, used all his athlete's strength and just pushed them all down the stairs, except what if somebody fell and broke a leg? They had enough problems as it was. "Hurry up," Bobby whispered. "Get going. What is taking so long?"

He could not tell whether he was talking out loud or not.

Outside, he thought, all I want is to be outside.

Sherree, incredibly, began taunting the vanished vampire. "You did-n't get us," she called, singsong. "We're go-ing ho-ome. Nan-ny nan-ny boo boo."

Why, Roxanne asked herself, were people like Sherree allowed on the planet? Enough of this, thought Roxanne. I have to get home and scrub off an entire layer of skin.

Roxanne shoved through the silly delaying pack and plunged forward.

Her brain turned into a mental map of the mansion. Nothing mattered but exits and speed.

First set of stairs, she thought. Turn right in upper hall. Go down second set of stairs. Turn at bottom. Enter abandoned dining room. Go through window. Reach porch. Run like the very —

But she could no longer run.

She could no longer move at all.

She had collided with the vampire.

Or his cloak.

It was not like running into a wet sheet hanging out to dry on a clothesline. It was more like sinking into the mud of low tide. The stench and vapor of the vampire hit Roxanne's face, filling her open mouth and her nostrils as if she had fallen into pudding.

I refuse to let this happen! thought Roxanne. She shoved both hands forward, with all her might, to push him out of her escape route.

Her hands went right through his body.

"I'm not entirely here yet," the vampire explained. "It's because I need a meal. I'm becoming extremely hungry, you know. It's all this time you are wasting. All this running around you're forcing me to do."

The vampire had begun walking up the stairs.

Bobby, Zach, Sherree, Randy, and Roxanne were forced to back up also.

Roxanne, coughing and spitting, tried to wipe the vampire off her face.

Sherree was sobbing and beating on Randy with her fists. "Tell him to stop this!" she said. "He's earned his money. Fire him, Randy!"

The vampire continued to sweep them up the stairs.

Sherree thinks it's an act, thought Lacey. How astonishing. All this evidence and she still does not believe in vampires.

Lacey stood her ground. She hung onto the railing and dug her sneakers into the stair treads. "We are not going back in your tower," she said. "It does not matter how hard you shove. We are not moving back up those stairs."

But the five other teenagers moved around Lacey the way water moves around a rock in the stream. Backward, up the narrow tower stairs they moved.

"Don't cooperate with him!" cried Lacey. "Don't go back in that tower. That's where his power is! Out here on this staircase, he can't do much."

"You are incorrect," said the vampire. He remained courteous.

Lacey did not. She aimed a savage kick at his shins.

But of course, he had not fully materialized, and like Roxanne, she found her foot entering a sort of gel that sucked and clung.

Lacey lost her balance, and fell back.

It was Randy who caught her, grabbing her under the arms, hauling her back against him, dragging her on up the stairs.

"All right!" shouted Sherree. "All right! I believe in you! It's okay. Don't get mad! We'll talk. We'll do anything you want!"

The vampire's chuckle was like broken glass, crunching under their shoes.

"No!" screamed Lacey, fighting Randy. "Don't go back in there! Stay out of that tower! We can hold him off! There's strength in numbers!" Lacey hung onto the banisters.

"You have a discussion to complete, as I recall," said the vampire. "The rules were made quite clear to you."

"We are not going to have a discussion on any subject whatsoever!" screamed Lacey. "We are going home!" Lacey grabbed at the retreating bodies of the others, trying to force them to stand next to her. What is the matter with them? she thought. Don't they understand?

"Regrettably," said the vampire, sounding rather like a guidance counselor, "due to Lacey's interfering and unpleasant manner, I am not going to be able to facilitate your discussion after all."

"Push your way through!" shrieked Lacey. "Don't — "

But the vampire rose up the stairs like fog rolling in from the sea.

His misty blanket enveloped them in his gelatinous pollution and they could not breathe under it, or near it, and they staggered back into the tower.

The weird sick light of the vampire illuminated the round space.

Roxanne thought she would drown in the vampire's smell. When will I ever be able to wash this off? she thought. She began to sob.

Zach's trembling began again, even deeper and more complete than it had been before. Bobby felt his mind leaving his skull, felt himself dividing, floating, coming apart. Randy felt terror filling his body; it was inside him, slithering around.

The tower seemed smaller than before.

Or else the vampire was taking up more space than he had.

"You made it worse, Lacey," Sherree said furiously.

"I did not make it worse!" cried Lacey. "It can't get any worse!"

"If I had just moved faster," sobbed Sherree, "I'd be out of here by now."

"There is," said the vampire, "only one way to get out of here."

His voice silenced them. They looked up. They saw. The vampire's face was present now, his skin the color of mushrooms. His teeth were as green as seaweed. He wiped them against his sleeve until they were white once more.

Sherree whimpered like a kicked puppy.

"The way out," said the vampire, "is not through a door."

The vampire's teeth filled more and more of his mouth. "The way out," said the vampire, "is not through a window."

"What way, then?" cried Sherree. "I'll do anything. Just tell me how to get out."

"You must choose my victim," repeated the vampire. He smiled. The teeth slid over his lips and touched his chin. "Although you have not discussed the issue as I requested, I think you all know, if you consider it for a moment, who has caused the most trouble here."

Sherree nodded. Without the slightest hesitation, she said, "I nominate Lacey."

"She's not running for office!" shouted Roxanne. "You don't nominate her."

"Yes, I do. The vampire wants a name, and that's what nominate means. I name Lacey." Sherree was calm. Relaxed. She was comfortable with her decision.

Sherree's calm spread through the tower just as the vampire's stench had. Bobby's mind seemed to return. Zach's trembling lessened. Randy's terror dwindled. Roxanne's anger quieted.

They looked at Lacey.

And the vampire, too. The vampire looked at Lacey.

"Lacey," repeated the vampire, as if tasting the syllables before he tasted the victim. "*Lacey.*"

Sherree is giving me to him, thought Lacey.

She was unable to believe it. She had been sure they would stick together as a group. But no. Darwin was correct. Survival of the fittest. What it meant was — throw out one member to save the rest.

How primitive humankind is, thought Lacey.

How sophisticated the vampire is compared to our species. We cannot last a night without caving in. He can last for years, without food, without light, without anything.

The vampire's eyes were soft and yearning. They fixed on Lacey, but did not meet her stare. The vampire was studying her throat.

Lacey waited for sturdier minds to kick in. Roxanne. Zachary. Bobby. She doubted if anybody could count on Randy in a crisis. Clearly not Sherree. But the rest . . . they would come through for her. They would not abandon her. Not to this. They would save her! She knew they would!

"Probably not, my dear," said the vampire gently, reading her thoughts. "It is always a shock to learn how cruel one's supposed friends can be."

Lacey wrenched her eyes off the vampire.

She turned to witness the actions of her supposed friends.

Sherree was already out the tower door.

Bobby's head was tilted slightly. He drew his glance away from Lacey, and then he drew himself to the tower door.

Roxanne massaged her wrists, as if she had sprained them. She was pouring her attention into her own body — carefully, calculatedly, forgetting Lacey's body.

Zach smiled at her nervously. He seemed embarrassed. And ready to go.

They had accepted Sherree's nomination.

Without speaking, they had voted.

Lacey's mind was flat and without words or thoughts. Perhaps this was how newborn babies were, before words and knowledge and experience were acquired to fill the void. Lacey so completely could not believe the other five were abandoning her, that her mind abandoned itself rather than accept the truth.

The vampire drifted slightly closer. His fangs seemed to lengthen, like fence posts coming out of the ground.

The five safe teenagers moved through the door.

"Don't start till I'm gone," said Sherree to the vampire.

The vampire laughed. It sounded like glass breaking on stone. Little glittery sharp pieces of death, falling out of the vampire's mouth, landing in a pile of used laughter at Lacey's feet.

But my life, thought Lacey. My plans. My family. My hopes.

She was unable to back away from the vampire. Unable to try to join the others. Was terror rooting her to the spot, or had the vampire already reached her, so that she, too, was simply waiting for Sherree to be gone, so the real evening could begin?

Nobody said good-bye.

Perhaps it was too normal a word.

Perhaps you did not say good-bye when you were consigning a friend to hell. Perhaps you just slithered away, like the snake you were.

Lacey could no longer watch them go.

She could only watch the vampire come.

Chapter 9

The cloak of the vampire moved by itself.

It swirled toward Lacey.

Perhaps it had muscles and a will of its own. Perhaps it was the real vampire. Perhaps the thing inside the cloak was but a mirage.

Lacey's eyes opened wider and wider. And yet she could see less and less, for the cloak of the vampire filled the entire room, its hem sweeping the ceiling and the floor together.

Her muscles yanked together, demanding action, but instead of running or fighting, Lacey stiffened and could not move.

Mom! she thought. Dad! Kevin!

The cloak rippled in symmetrical folds. It was a wet dripping thing to line caves. And in another moment, it would encircle her; she would be nothing but "an event" to this cape.

I won't cry, thought Lacey. I won't whimper or moan. I certainly will not scream, because he said he liked that best.

But she knew that she would scream. The scream

was building up in the bottom of her lungs, and demanding release, the scream was a living creature all by itself, and it, too, was climbing. She could feel the scream erupting like a latent volcano.

Would they hear? The five who had left her here? Would they hear her scream? Would it chill their hearts?

But they don't have hearts, thought Lacey. If they had hearts, they would not have left me here.

The corners of the vampire's cloak curled up, like fingers.

Dripping, the fingers crept toward her.

Sherree was the first one out the door. The first to put a foot on the top step of the stairs. The first to grab the banister and taste the wonderful freedom that waited outside the mansion.

Sherree envisioned the great outdoors. The real world. The acceptable, ordinary world of normal people doing normal things.

A world in which you could worry about what to wear, and how to accessorize, and with whom to flirt. A world in which you could do homework, or watch television, or drive a car.

A safe world.

Sherree put her mind into that safe world, that world without slime and without terror.

But her mind would not go.

Her mind stayed with Lacey.

Lacey. Alone with that *thing*? What would it be like for Lacey? Alone? No human beside her? Just Lacey and Evil?

For Sherree, to whom parties and friends and crowds and ringing telephones were life, to be alone was the greatest curse of all.

Lacey is alone, thought Sherree.

I nominated her to be alone.

Forever and ever.

This is like the sinking of the *Titanic*, thought Roxanne. Survivors didn't even wait for enough passengers to fill the lifeboat; they just rowed away, listening to the screams of the drowning — who could easily have fit into their half-empty boat.

I'm leaving Lacey, thought Roxanne. This girl with whom I was supposed to be at a party. Laughing. Dancing. Joking. The party went sour, but I went more sour. I left her there. Alone.

I'll be free. I'll be safe. But not unless I row away from a drowning friend.

Roxanne thought of the high school yearbook. What would they write about Roxanne, after twelve years of school in the same town?

A flamboyant personality! A girl of vast talent and a brilliant future! But of course . . . in the end . . . Roxanne was the first to abandon ship. Let somebody else drown! said Roxanne. I'll take the lifeboat, thank you. (That was Roxanne's motto. Who needs Lacey, anyway? Show me the door. That was our friend Roxanne.)

Roxanne took another step down. And then another. At the same time, the vampire must be taking another step toward Lacey. And then another.

Would Lacey scream?

Would Roxanne hear that scream all the nights of her life?

Bobby had not really been thinking. Being pinned to the wall had left him with the strength of a laboratory specimen. He had just sort of been lying on a table, ready for dissection. He was there, and his shape was no different, but his mind had been dulled.

The only thing that had penetrated the curtain of fear was his athletic training. Team sports. Through the gluey thickness of his mind, Bobby had a sense that he had let his team down. But what was the team? What was the sport? Who was the player?

Bobby had a sense that he was moving the wrong way down the court. He was going to make a basket for the opposite team. Wait, he thought. Wait. Look around. What is the strategy here? Whose team am I on?

Zach's mind, however, was sharpened by fear. He could readily imagine the vampire wanting to renegotiate that contract of his. Would Lacey be enough for the vampire? What if the vampire was not satisfied by Lacey alone?

Sherree plowed to a stop. For one horrible moment Zach thought the vampire had changed his mind, and had once again taken possession of the stairs. That "escape" had all been a cruel joke. *Nobody would escape.* Not now. Not ever.

"Hurry up, Sherree!" Zach didn't want the vampire to realize how slowly they were leaving. Who knew how quickly the vampire's "event" with Lacey could take place? What if it happened in the few seconds they wasted getting downstairs? What if Lacey merely whetted the vampire's appetite and the vampire followed them down?

Zach did not want to be last in line.

The thing was to get down the stairs, get out that dining room window, get off the sagging porch, and get off this property. As far as Zach was concerned, Randy's Land Rover could be abandoned until daylight. Or forever. Zach was going to hit the grass running.

And yet his feet hardly moved.

At the back of his mind, at the heels of his escape, he saw Lacey. ·

Alone.

A sick taste rose up in his throat. He told himself it was the atmosphere in the mansion. Horror had a flavor and an aroma all its own.

But he knew in his heart that the truly horrible event of the night was not what the vampire intended to do.

The horror was himself.

Leaving Lacey.

Randy saw an opening between Zach and Roxanne and slipped through, moving to the head of the pack, catching up with Sherree. The house was a pit of blackness below the tower, but Randy could see perfectly. He could see freedom and safety and his life reemerging. He could see clean air and hear the quick start of his car's engine. In one minute, he would be driving away and never thinking about this again.

That would be the key, of course. Never to think about this again.

Because if you thought about it . . .

Randy thought about it.

With all his inner strength, he tried not to, but Randy did not have great inner strength. In fact, here on the stairs, he knew that he possessed nothing but weakness.

Randy had invited to this party nothing but a collection of egos. Selfish, selfish people.

Roxanne: the selfish achiever.

Sherree: the selfish beauty.

Bobby: the selfish jock.

Zachary: the selfish classy act.

Randy himself: the selfish hanger-on.

And Lacey.

Randy could not believe he had ever let anybody call her a dwindle-head. What was a dwindle-head, anyway? He was. They all were.

I invited Lacey here, thought Randy. She's here because I asked her to come.

How to treat your date, he thought hysterically. Give her the night of her life.

I offered her, thought Sherree. Those were my words. *I nominate Lacey.* I cannot live with that.

I didn't even argue, thought Roxanne. I would have seconded the motion if the vampire had asked me to.

I can't do this, thought Zach. If there's any test in life, this is it. I can't fail it. I can't fail Lacey.

I'm half the vampire's anyway, thought Bobby. I should be the one he takes. He's got some of me anyhow.

Sherree turned. Bobby turned. Roxanne turned. Zach turned. But they were not the first. Randy had already raced back into the tower. "Stop!" he shouted. "Don't touch her!"

Randy flung his arms around Lacey.

Lacey was untouched.

The vampire, after all, had not moved quickly. Why let pleasure evaporate before he had had time to enjoy it fully?

Only the cloak had changed position. Only the fangs had lengthened.

"Take me instead," said Randy.

The vampire's fangs vanished behind his lips. The lips drew into a thin bloodless line and tucked themselves into his face and disappeared.

Randy was filled with glory and pride. "Take me," he repeated, and his voice sounded rich and splendid in his own ears. "I dare you."

Lacey could have wept.

Randy. Volunteering to sacrifice himself. Randy, whom she had found the most useless in the group. She did not love him. Perhaps nothing could command the emotion of love. Perhaps love had to arrive on its own. But he had redeemed himself.

I am all right, she thought. *Randy came back*.

The cloak jerked away as if it had been attacked and wrapped itself tightly around the vampire.

Randy's forearm was in front of Lacey. She looked down at its classic pose: man slaying dragon for fair maiden. Oh, Randy! she thought. You are so far away from being a dragon-slayer. But you slew him anyway.

The room filled with humans instead of sick evil cloaks. "We came back!" shouted Roxanne.

"We're not scumbags after all!" cried Sherree.

The girls pushed Randy away and hugged Lacey themselves, laughing and proud. "We were decent in the end," said Roxanne.

Lacey did not tell them how terrible it had been for her; how their desertion had hurt her more than any vampire's fang ever could. Lacey did not tell them how it felt to be utterly alone: alone forever. She looked at Roxanne and Sherree and she let them be proud. She said softly, "Yes. You were decent in the end."

She wondered if that was enough. Did it erase doing something very bad, if you rushed back and undid it as quickly as you could? Or were you stained by that bad thing? Was it part of you now, like a scar on your heart?

The vampire, flushed like a bird from a thicket, fluttered around the room. He did not leave, although he became more shadow than substance.

Randy, standing taller, feeling broader, feeling better than ever before in his life, shouted, "What are you — a coward? You can't take me on after all? I volunteer. Understand that, vampire?"

The vampire's voice creaked like an old floor under their feet. It scratched their souls like chalk on a blackboard. "You won't be a hero," said the vampire. "You do realize that, don't you, Randy?"

"I'm not trying to be one," said Randy, who of course was trying very hard. Who had already decided he was a hero. Who had already reworked his entire life plan, so that he would be a hero in everything now, always. What would he do next? He had saved Lacey, perhaps next he would save the world. It was simply a matter of choosing which enemy to whip. Would it be global politics or virus research or —

"Ah, sixteen," said the vampire, returning to his original subject. "A dangerous age. This is, I suppose, a moral equivalent of pushing the accelerator to the floor. You, little Randy, will run the farthest, you will scurry the fastest, to save your little friend."

His voice was condescending: the adult who understood reality in a roomful of children who did not. His smile reemerged. This time all the teeth were pointed, and neatly aligned, as if something had redrawn them; as if a new, and more calculating, vampire was going to fill the room.

Randy felt a puncture wound in his side: not from the vampire, but from some new horror yet to be explained.

He stared as one, and only one, of the fangs, lengthened.

It seemed to pierce his strength, his determination, his resolve.

The old selfish Randy — who had vanished only moments ago — began to grow back. No! thought

Randy. No! Please — let me be a hero!

"You see," said the vampire, comfortably, like an old armchair, "you will not be a hero because your friends will forget the events of the night as they pass out of the building. They will retain no memory of you, Randy. No memory of me, either. No memory at all."

It's true, thought Roxanne. I had already forgotten that I am covered with vampire slime. I had already forgotten that I have to scour myself clean and bake in the sun to get rid of his leavings. I had already forgotten that I lay in his nest. I, Roxanne, was contaminated by his actual lair. And I forgot that in those few steps down the stairs. If we had gone just a few more steps, *we would have forgotten Lacey.* Out of sight, out of mind. We would not have felt guilty because we would not have remembered there was an "event" to worry about.

"Otherwise, of course," added the vampire, "your friends would get fire trucks and police and who knows what? Obviously that cannot be allowed. So they will not remember. And a person who is forgotten, my dear Randy, cannot be a hero. A hero, by definition, is one whom his friends adore."

"He is a hero," said Lacey steadily. "They are all heroes. They came back. They did not run. And *that* is the definition of a hero."

The vampire's eyes grew larger and clearer. He studied Lacey with as much interest as he had before. "There is another interesting reality," he said. A second fang grew down to meet the first. How could he talk with his teeth shifting like that? And yet, the voice hardly seemed to come from the mouth at all. It came from the entire room.

"Nobody's interested in your dumb old realities," said Randy. He flung his head back. He spread his legs. He jammed his hands into his pockets, as if he had guns in holsters, and would beat the vampire to the draw. "I don't even think you can really do this, anyway," sneered Randy. "I don't think there's any such thing as an 'event.' You're nothing but a slimeball. Maybe I'm not a hero. But you're not a vampire, either. You're just a thing without power."

The darkness in the room became entire.

The vampire gave off no phosphorescence.

The room was utterly silent.

They could hear no breathing. They could see no cloak. They dared not move, because they could not see their feet, nor the gaping hole in the floor that Roxanne had created.

Roxanne could not help it. She wrapped one arm around the back of her neck.

Sherree, tightly clinging to somebody's hand, suddenly wondered just whose hand it was she held. Was it a human hand?

Randy called the vampire's bluff. "I'm waiting," he said.

Chapter 10

"Aw, come on, Ginny, lighten up," said Jordan.

Ginny was at a crossroads with Jordan, literally and figuratively. They could turn onto the valley road, and head for the Mall House, or they could go on to their friends' house where they were expected.

It was, thought Ginny, so annoying that you could not just go out for the evening. Everything always had to involve some sort of choice. Some sort of principle.

All Ginny wanted was friends and pizza. A little company, a few laughs.

Instead, she had a boyfriend problem.

If she said, "No, Jordan, we're going to the party, forget this driving-around-and-hunting-for-my-brother nonsense," was she simply asserting her rights in this relationship, or was she bossing Jordan around?

If she said, "Okay, Jordan, whatever you want, Jordan," was she being good company and lightening up, or was she being a doormat on whom Jordan would scrape his shoes forevermore?

Ginny was aware that one of her biggest personality problems was a tendency to analyze too often.

Of course, one of Jordan's biggest personality problems was that he never analyzed anything at all.

What we need here, thought Ginny, is a compromise.

Ginny frowned, climbing into her brain cells, hunting for a satisfactory compromise.

The problem was, Ginny didn't like compromising. Ginny liked having her own way.

"I can't idle at this intersection for our whole lives, you know," remarked Jordan.

"Why not?" said Ginny. "There's no traffic tonight."

Jordan nodded in a slow, thoughtful way. "I don't understand that, either," he said. "Saturday night at this hour? There should be all kinds of cars going by, especially right here, and right now." Jordan fluttered his hands like a passing ghost. "Perhaps," he said, in a deep ghoulish voice, "there are other forces at work tonight."

"Perhaps," said Ginny, letting herself get drawn in, "my little brother has been absorbed by an evil being."

"No doubt," said Jordan. He rolled down the window of his car. "In fact," he whispered, "the very air is redolent of evil."

Ginny rolled down her window.

A strange thick smell sifted into their car.

It was not car exhaust.

Ginny did not know what it was. She only knew she was beginning to prickle all over with fear. "Jordan?" she whispered.

Jordan was staring out the window he had just opened.

His eyes were open far too wide. His hands had fallen off the steering wheel. His breath was coming in strange little spurts.

Ginny looked where he was looking.

Down the valley road. Down where once the hemlocks had towered around the old house with the twisted tower. Down where someday a parking lot would lie flat and black against the ground.

The tower was visible against the sooty sky.

And from the tower came curving, slinking squares of blackness like immense pieces of paper, curving and reshaping themselves.

The smell grew worse.

Ginny felt her lungs tiring, her heart slowing.

Jordan's hands went back on the wheel. Jordan's foot lifted from the brake. The automatic transmission moved the car forward, slowly at first, and then gathering momentum. Jordan was not quite steering and not quite touching the gas pedal. The car was going down the valley road, going all by itself toward the black shape that lowered gently, as if to meet them.

Ginny thought: Nobody will come to look for *us*. Because we're supposed to be the ones doing the looking.

"As I say," repeated the vampire, "there is another interesting reality."

Randy tried to glare at the vampire, but it was difficult. The vampire did not stay in one place, and the parts of him that materialized changed each time.

"You see," said the vampire, "being a hero is a human reality. It is not part of my world. And it is within my world that we operate tonight."

"What are you talking about?" said Lacey. Could it really be correct that the six teenagers would retain no memory of the night's events? How terrible that would be! Randy's wonderful courage — lost like a fog burning off in the morning sun. Her own shattering fear — vanished like pain from a paper cut. This new deep knowledge of each other; this new view into the depths and the shallowness of five others — evaporated.

Would Lacey really not know Sherree, nor Zach, nor Roxanne, nor Bobby when school opened on Monday? Would they really be strangers to her as they had been strangers before? And Randy . . .

What would Randy be?

There would be less of him, the vampire had said. Not dead, and yet gone. Still breathing, and yet lacking personality.

And would she, Lacey, for whom he had sacrificed, even know about it? Would she ignore him in the halls? Not see him in the cafeteria? Not care about him on the bus? Would Randy be faceless?

Even though he had endured this horrible fate by choice, for their sake?

Lacey did weep, after all.

At least Randy saw that. At least Randy had a moment of tears.

And then she wondered — would *Randy* remember?

Would Randy be a zombie, staggering dimly through the remaining years of his life, lacking even the comfort of his own courage? Or would terrible knowledge lie within him — useless, unspoken?

"My world," said the vampire, very soft, very low. "In my world, you will recall, you had to choose my victim from among you. Randy has volunteered instead. And this, of course, saves him. Randy can no longer be my victim." The vampire smiled. In his voice as rich as dark chocolate, he murmured, "I neglected to explain to you that a person who volunteers to sacrifice himself for others . . ." and here, the vampire smiled, a smile so full of teeth it seemed that there were several vampires living in his mouth, " . . . is always safe. You may leave if you wish, Randy."

Randy stared at the vampire. What was going on? What had happened to his great bravery, his sacrifice, his splendor?

With a swirl of his cloak, the vampire discarded Randy. "You are out of the running, Randy. Very clever of you. Very self-serving."

Randy felt the world being yanked out from under his feet. "I didn't volunteer to be clever," he protested. He wanted to be a hero. He wanted to be applauded and lauded like athletes after great victories: like Bobby, for example.

"No," said the vampire gently, knowing Randy's mind, "those are the daydreams of humans. They are not the realities of vampires."

Lacey was glad that Randy was safe. She had seen the best in Randy, and she wanted Randy to continue on that road; to be good and worthy and generous of heart. She smiled, looked down for privacy in her thoughts, and smiled again. At least something good would come from this.

"Randy is safe?" repeated Zach.

"He is safe," agreed the vampire.

Zach, Sherree, Bobby, and Roxanne studied Randy in his new role as the safe one; the one who would go free; the one who would definitely get home tonight. They felt a strange rage at Randy, because he was no longer part of the group; he had been removed to another zone.

"The field," said the vampire, "is narrowed. There are now five remaining choices for me. Five," he repeated greedily. "Five. Five. Five. Five."

Lacey's shudder was deep in her gut, but she knew that the vampire was aware of it, and enjoying it, and hoping there would be more.

Only Sherree moved logically to the next point. "Heck," said Sherree, "then I volunteer, too."

"Thank you, my dear," said the vampire. His eyes softened with dreamy pleasure and his largest teeth slid over his damp lips and hooked at the bottom of his chin. "You may all go now. Except Sherree, of course. Most thoughtful of you to resolve the situation, Sherree." The tongue that licked his lips was pointed like a red ribbon. He moved far more swiftly to Sherree than he had toward Lacey.

"Wait!" screamed Lacey, grabbing Sherree's arm and yanking her back. "This isn't fair! You keep changing the rules."

"I am not changing the rules at all," said the vampire. His breath came in spurts, like whiffs of swamp gas. "You just don't know them. I can't help it that you are not acquainted with the workings of my world. I have certainly taken the time to become acquainted with *your* world."

The vampire's cloak encircled Sherree's arm. It began to haul her in, as if she were clothes on an old-fashioned clothesline, being reeled onto the back porch. From beneath the folds of his horrible wrappings came his fingernails, like crushed foil, and then his hands, longer than human hands, bonier than human hands, stronger than human hands.

Sherree screamed in horror. The vampire was ecstatic. Screams were his appetizers.

"Wait!" said Lacey. She had one of Sherree's arms and the cloak had the other. "Wait. I have to think."

"You may think outdoors," said the vampire. "It's time for the five of you to go."

"No!" shouted Lacey. "You said to start with that *we* had to choose your victim. Well, we didn't! You broke the rules. This does not count."

"Sherree volunteered for selfish purposes. I accepted. It's not frequent for a victim to request being taken, but it is not unknown in history," said the vampire, "and I am content with it."

Sherree broke free both from the vampire's cloak and from Lacey. She ran in circles around the diminishing tower. There were no exits. Once again, the vampire possessed the door. Ripping mindlessly at the remaining shutters blocking the tower windows, Sherree tried to find a way out of her fate. Her strength far surpassed even Bobby's, fueled by adrenaline from her deathly fear.

Gradually her frenzy diminished.

Gradually her crazed attempts ceased.

And yet the vampire did not approach her. His head was cocked as if he had ears hidden beneath his horrid oily hair, as if he were listening to something.

They all listened.

Somewhere in the house, somebody was laughing.

The policewoman was bored.

Night duty was often boring.

She did not actually want anything to happen, and yet if she were to stay awake, something had to happen. She drank from the take-out paper cup of coffee. It was chilly now. Pretty awful stuff. But she had nothing else to do, so she sipped again.

The policewoman was quite young. She had graduated from the local high school not so long ago herself.

One-handed, she drove through the dark and quiet town. There used to be a lot more action on this side of the city, but since so many acres had been cleared for the future shopping mall, there was not much here. She paused at an intersection and considered driving past the old boarded-up mansion.

When the policewoman had been in high school, she had been a cheerleader, and had briefly known the girl who lived in that mansion. There had been parties there. Parties at which everybody seemed to know more than they let on. Parties from which people seemed to come and go as if they could move through walls. And then the girl herself had gone, as quickly and quietly as if she, too, had been walled up.

When the house was abandoned, nobody had ever gone there.

It was odd.

You would think — certainly the police force expected — that the teenagers of the town would see this as an ideal hangout.

But nobody had tried spending the night in its abandoned rooms. Nobody had spun wheelies in its pathetic old gardens, and nobody had written a six-foot-high CLASS OF '95 in red paint on its sagging roof.

The policewoman had had a tumultuous high school career herself. There was not much she had not done, or tried, or at least watched. It was one reason she went into law enforcement: she was pretty familiar with the mood or the need that made a person break the laws. She was stern now, but she understood.

There was no traffic. Really, it was remarkable.

And on a weekend! Where were all the partying teenagers? The drunks who should be plastered by this time? The moviegoers who should be headed home after the late show?

The police car edged forward, as only police cars can, taking its eternal time, because nobody can argue.

But there were no other cars in sight that would mind the delay.

Balancing the awful coffee, she approached the intersection of the valley road and the main downtown avenue.

The bright red taillights of a single car crept down the valley road and vanished.

The policewoman wondered whose driveway could possibly be down there. For a moment she waited, to see if the taillights would reappear, as a very lost driver backed out of a very unpromising drive.

But none appeared.

Truly, the night was dead.

In lieu of any other action, the policewoman decided to go to the drive-in window of Dunkin Donuts. A jelly doughnut, she pondered, or a glazed cruller?

The police car turned the opposite direction from the twisted tower. The policewoman was not looking in her rearview mirror to see what was happening there.

But it would not have mattered if she had looked.

For vampires do not have reflections.

* * *

Sherree was swinging on one of the shutters, as if to hurl herself through the window, through the night, and come to a safe landing miles away.

The laugh shivered through the cracks in the plaster and came up through the cracks in the floorboards. It lay in the attic and it slid off the roof and it collapsed in the basement.

The laugh wrapped them like a gift box.

Except that the laugh was evil.

"Do vampires laugh?" said Zach. Zach did not sound as if he would ever laugh again.

"Vampires laugh," said the vampire, "when they have a victim in sight. Other than that, it is quite rare."

The shutters clattered.

All their little wooden slats clapped.

Sherree slid down from the shutter to which she had clung and fell in a heap on the floor.

A second vampire entered the tower.

Chapter 11

Two vampires, thought Lacey.

It was beyond thinking about. She seemed to have no mind left. She could draw no conclusions and take no action. She could only stare.

The first vampire — Lacey could not stop herself from thinking of him as *their* vampire — was so much more cloak than this new one. This new one was gelatinous, sticky and dark like molasses dripping on a floor.

Once when Lacey was quite small she and her father had been working in the garden, only to push the sharp edge of a shovel right down into a ground wasps' nest. There had been a very brief moment in which wasps had zoomed out of their hole, circled once, and then attacked Lacey and her father. Lacey had not even known what a wasp was, but she knew enough to run.

Her father scooped her up as he fled, and they flew like rockets to the back door, slamming it against the buzzing horrors that followed them. Between them, Lacey and her father got eleven wasp bites.

We've found a vampires' nest, thought Lacey. We pushed the sharp edge of the shovel down into the ground where vampires live.

What had really happened to the families who had lived in this house? Had they actually moved away? Or had something truly terrible happened to them? Had they hung wallpaper on a wall, only to learn who lived behind it? Had they dusted a shutter only to find the dark ooze of evil coming off on their innocent hands?

Tear it down! thought Lacey. Tear this house down! This house must be ended. Once the house is gone, these vampires must surely also be gone.

Facing two vampires was infinitely more terrifying than facing one.

Their vampire stood by the door he possessed. The new vampire blocked the shutters. Beyond him, since Sherree had yanked open all the shutters, the night sky was exposed. It was black. Nothing hung there, not a star, not a distant plane. Only blackness.

The vampire had told the truth. Inside this house, night would last as long as he needed it to.

Perhaps the house would never be torn down; perhaps the vampire could control even time, and the time to build the shopping mall would never come, and the time for rescue and the time to go home — these would never come, either.

Zach and Roxanne kept swivelling their heads. They seemed to think as long as they kept an eye on each vampire, nothing could happen.

The vampire who had emerged from the shutters eventually stopped laughing. The laughter had poured out of him like water from a faucet, and Lacey had wanted just to turn him off, like a knob, and be done listening to his noise.

Sherree, whose flesh the new vampire had brushed, kept making faces and gagging and crying, "*Eeeeeuuuuuuuhhhh!*"

Bobby stared out the window, as if expecting somebody else to come in, some shape or horror not yet envisioned.

Only Randy seemed untouched by the new circumstance. He, after all, could not be prey. The rest were now, as the vampire had said early in the evening, simply small animals about to be taken by larger ones. But Randy was out of the running.

The vampires did not seem to be friends. Perhaps vampires did not have friends. And although they had long resided in the same house, one living between the floors, and the other living between the shutters, it seemed that they had not met in many years. Their schedules, it seemed, and their need for nourishment, did not coincide.

For the second vampire was starving. He had been closed up, he said, for a long, long time.

Zach said, "You're the one who peeled my fingers off the sill, aren't you?"

The vampire was pleased to be recognized.

"Eeeeuuuhh, he touched you, too?" said Sherree. "Eeeeuuuhh, this is so sick."

Roxanne suddenly giggled. Sherree kept adding

touches of human reality. It gave Roxanne a divided sensation, as if she had been split down the middle like a piece of pie: she was half in the vampire's world and half in Sherree's.

This is not real, thought Roxanne. This is either a really weird party or a really weird nightmare, but this is not real. It relaxed her greatly to reassure herself that this was not real.

"Why did you do that?" said Zach.

"I didn't expect to be awakened," said the new vampire. "Naturally I was annoyed to find human fingers all over my shutters. But now that I am up, I recall that it was time anyhow. Our building will be removed from this world in only a week. I have things to do. A new home to find. A nest to build."

The old vampire nodded glumly. "They are wiping out our habitats."

Zach burst out laughing, a response that obviously pleased him, because it sounded normal and in control. "You sound like environmentalists," said Zach. "As if we should preserve a forest for you. Or at least a cemetery."

The new vampire looked with distaste at Zach. (Zach felt this was probably the best way to be looked at by a vampire.) "You allow them to speak like this in your presence?" the new vampire said to theirs. "This generation is most unpleasant. They have no reverence for the old ways."

Their own vampire smiled. "They will," he said. His soft eyes landed especially on Roxanne, who had been pretending this was a bad dream.

"By dawn," whispered the vampire, looking so

deeply into her eyes it felt as if he could see down into her throat, "they will have respect for us again."

Both vampires were lost in thought over this probability.

"No, we won't," said Lacey. "I don't know where on earth you could get the idea that anybody would respect you. We all despise you. So there."

The vampires regarded Lacey steadily.

Then they faced each other. "I would like to finish up in here all by myself, if you don't mind," said their vampire. "But there is no need for you to go hungry. You need only slip outdoors. There are more humans waiting in the yard."

"Just standing there?" said the shutter vampire. "Waiting to be taken?" He rubbed his bones together. They clacked. They sounded just like the shutter slats.

Lacey thought perhaps they *were* the shutter slats. No wonder the previous occupants of this house had gone insane. Shutters made of vampire bones.

"Why is the house suddenly so popular?" mused the shutter vampire. His eyebrows were hairy and pointed, like fur-trimmed church windows.

"My understanding," said their vampire, "is that younger humans enjoy being frightened. It's the age, you know. Sixteen. Dangerous. To them, of course. Not us."

The second vampire smiled so broadly that his teeth seemed to circle his skull. "How touching," he said.

"Precisely."

"I shall be off then," said the second vampire. "I must plunge in," he added. He liked this turn of phrase, and he watched the teenagers as each one slowly understood the pun—what the plungers were, and into what they plunged.

But the vampire of the shutters did not go out of the window yet. Instead, he studied the six with a sort of melancholy; a kind of deep longing. "You aren't really going to let five of them go, are you?"

The first vampire nodded.

"I suppose that was a promise?" said the vampire of the shutters, sadly.

"It was merely *my* promise," said the first vampire. "*You* didn't make it."

Mardee had had it.

First of all, even though they could see the Land Rover right there, they could not reach the vehicle. It was surrounded by these stupid fallen trees. And they weren't little piddly Christmas trees you could just drag off. They were immense, as big as ranch houses. How on earth had the others gotten that vehicle in there, anyway?

Mardee snagged her legs and her ankles and her hair in every single hemlock branch there was.

Kevin, of course, was unscathed.

I will never associate with a boy again, Mardee told herself.

Mardee's brother Bobby was a total annoyance in her life. His friends and teammates were even more annoying. Given this depressing exposure to the opposite sex, Mardee had never been willing to give boys much of a chance. People said things looked up after eighth grade, and boys became human, but Mardee had seen no signs of this in her brother Bobby.

So here she had taken a chance on Kevin, because he had such a sensible sister — Lacey — and all Kevin would do was laugh at her, accuse her of screaming, and lead her into thickets of scraping, vicious, dead trees.

"You said on the phone," Kevin reminded her, "that we would come over here and make noise and frighten the kids inside."

"The *noise*," said Mardee frigidly, "*came* from inside. It was probably your very own sister, whom you are *deserting*."

"Deserting," said Kevin, delighted with the pun he was about to utter, "in order to have dessert. Come on. Let's go get ice cream. Nobody's here."

"Have you forgotten what just happened?" shouted Mardee.

Kevin stared at her, genuinely surprised to be yelled at.

And Mardee saw that, truly, Kevin had forgotten what had just happened. He did not remember the wet slimy mass that had slid past them, holding some terrible sobbing burden in its grasp. He did not remember the terrible force of its wake, the sucking wind that had yanked Mardee in through the window. He could no longer hear the moaning and the weeping that Mardee had heard coming all the way out of the earth, out of the soil, out of the cellar, out of the ages. He did not remember the cruel horrid laughters that sprang like opposite choruses of evil from the sky and the ground.

He had forgotten.

He was just a teenage boy, equally inspired by food or girls.

"Let's sit in the backseat of the Land Rover," said Kevin, leering.

Mardee favored him with a look of absolute loathing, but Kevin, being as stupid a boy as her brother Bobby, misinterpreted Mardee's look as one of agreement: that backseats and kisses were tops on her list, too.

Boys, thought Mardee.

She was getting in the Land Rover, all right, and then she was slamming the door and staying nice and safe in there until everybody came out from whatever ghastly party they were having inside and she didn't care what dumb old Kevin did. He could have all the ice cream on earth for all she cared.

Mardee climbed over the last interfering branch and grabbed the handle of the Land Rover.

Teeth glittered through the window.

Roxanne was the first to understand this new piece of information. "You mean, even if we get out," shrieked Roxanne, "even if you take only one of us, this other vampire can have more?" She could not believe this. A deal was a deal. What kind of game were these vampires playing?

"Perhaps if you make your choice more speedily," said the vampire, "my guest will still be busy with

124

the humans in the yard. Perhaps in that case, you will indeed escape notice by my guest."

Who on earth could be in the yard? thought Lacey. Who else was dumb enough to be here at this hour? In this terrible dark? With these horrible smells and atmospheres?

Lacey took swift steps to the open shutters. Grabbing the window rims, and leaning into the fresh air, she screamed out the window. "Run!" she shrieked, calling on every molecule of lung power. "Get out of here!"

There was no sound anywhere.

Not in the tower, not in the yard.

"Go away!" screamed Lacey. "Quick! Run!"

The vampire of the shutters said gently, "You are clearly not, although a human yourself, a student of human nature, my dear. When told to run, human beings inevitably stand still. When told to be afraid, human beings inevitably become curious instead. What you have done, of course, is merely to whet the appetites of those below." The vampire smiled, this time courteously covering his mouth. "And my appetite, too, of course."

He sifted between her and the windows. Lacey did not flinch. She would not give him the satisfaction.

The vampire evaporated, slowly, his eyes going first, then his flesh, then his teeth, and at last followed by his wrappings.

He drifted out the window rather like smoke from a fireplace, slow and thick and gray.

"And now," said their vampire, "let us finish up."

Chapter 12

The voice that screamed from the tower was his sister's.

It was Lacey.

Dwindle-head Lacey was, after all, partying in the mansion.

Kevin had never heard her scream like that. He had never heard anybody scream like that. The ferocity in her voice — *Run! Get out of here! Quick!* — stunned Kevin.

He could not worry about the person sitting in the Land Rover, whoever he was. He could not even worry about Mardee.

Mardee had actually fainted. Kevin had been thrilled. He had not known this happened in real life, either — girls passing out lightly in their boy-friends' arms. Of course, Mardee despised him, but on the other hand, he had caught her before she fell all the way, so perhaps that would count for something.

But he forgot Mardee. His hands didn't forget; they yanked her vertically to her feet, although this was not the proper reaction for dealing with faints. She became a simple burden to him, a thing to haul along, like schoolbooks down a hallway.

"Lace!" he shouted. "Lace!"

Nobody answered.

The house was silent.

Mardee had not actually fainted, just dropped down so that the vampire in the Land Rover would not see her so clearly. Now, clearly, she could see it was not a vampire at all, but some boy with bad teeth. Randy must have loaned his car to the guy.

This was definitely not the place for a girl with an overactive imagination. Mardee shook her head to clear it of idiocy. Perhaps it was Kevin's influence, seeing all this nonsense.

"We'll be out of your way in a moment," she said to the driver of the Land Rover. The guy gave her the creeps.

"She's in there," whispered Kevin, staring up at the tower.

Shutters banged. Down here among the dead trees there was no wind, but the wind at the rooftop must have been strong, for blackness seemed to dip and sway along the windows, as if the sky itself were casting a shadow on the mansion, and then taking it away.

"I heard her!" whispered Kevin.

"Told you so," said Mardee.

Boys drive me crazy, thought Mardee. I said to Kevin, I said, Lacey's in there. Your sister. And he said, Nah, let's go get ice cream. I said,

Kevin, there's a vampire in there. And he laughed at me. Now he's acting as if *he's* the only one who noticed that something is wrong!

Kevin tried to find his way out of the fallen trees. "I'm coming, Lacey!" he yelled.

"Alternatively," said the vampire, "you may all stay."

The room was absolutely quiet.

"After all," said the vampire, "if you each wish to experience this event, who am I to deny you?"

The thickness of his atmosphere was so great that they had difficulty breathing.

"I would think it more logical to choose one for me and save the rest, but if you feel you should all stay," said the vampire, and here his teeth seemed to point individually at each of them, "I am willing to work harder tonight. I am willing to work all night."

The vampire laughed.

Jordan's car steered into the driveway and stopped.

Jordan opened his door.

Ginny opened hers.

They got out.

The shadow in the sky drifted slowly down across the roofs, like a sleepwalker, and descended gently to the ground.

Yes, thought Ginny, not knowing what she was saying yes to, or why she felt that yes was the right syllable. Only knowing that something — some strange gravity — was pulling her toward that shadow. It was pulling Jordan, too, they were going in a pair.

Ginny wanted to call out, "Over here!" but she could not seem to move her lips.

She was not afraid, and yet she was terrorized. Her body was doing things without her, as if this had been rehearsed for all her life.

Jordan felt like paper. He was blank. Nothing was written on him. Nothing was on his last page and nothing would be on his next page.

He did not feel like a man or a boy or a human being.

He did not even feel.

He was hardly even there.

His feet continued to move, and yet he did not feel as if he were walking. He felt as if he had become some sort of amoeba, with jellied expansions instead of legs. He was floating in a new kind of water.

Whatever the shadow was, whatever the shadow meant, Jordan would be absorbed into it.

Yes, thought Jordan.

Lacey could hardly absorb the vampire's words, let alone the diluted oxygen left in the tower. That was my brother down there, thought Lacey. My brother, Kevin. What is he doing there? My brother, Kevin, who is going to be the other vampire's victim!

Lacey and Kevin had led remarkably separate lives for a brother and sister whose bedroom doors were separated by only thirty-six inches. They shared no hobbies, they had no common friends, they participated in none of the same activities. Since Lacey had become a teenager they had hardly even had dinner together, because her schedule was not similar to her brother's.

At family gatherings, like Thanksgiving, Lacey and Kevin sometimes discovered that they, too, were having a reunion. That they would actually have conversations in which Lacey would think — so this is the kind of guy that Kevin is! They would actually catch up on each other when the room was full of relatives, as if they, too, were distant cousins who saw each other only on holidays.

"Lace!" came her brother's voice from outside, from the safety zone, from the ground beneath the tower. "I'm coming, Lace!"

He did not call her Lace, instead of Lacey, because he was fond of her and this was a favorite nickname. He called her Lace because he was cutting down on the time he spent thinking of her; one less syllable spent on a dumb old sister.

For the same reason, she usually called him Kev.

We will each die, she thought. Well, no, not die. The vampire explained that death is not part of this. But we will be finished, as human beings.

Our poor parents. Tomorrow they will have half-children. Half-personalities. Half-energies.

We will live together in some sort of mental and physical fog, drained by the vampire, and we will not know. We will not remember.

Lacey stared at the vampire, imagining the

"event." The vampire stared back, also imagining it. Although with more enthusiasm.

It was evident that, this time, the vampire was not going to leave.

There would be no escape.

There would be no exit unless granted by the vampire.

And her brother was in the yard. Coming up into the house.

I must get my brother out of here, thought Lacey. And while I'm at it, I must save the rest.

Lacey examined the others. She was no longer in human time, but vampire time: time that continued for eons in a single black night. She did not have to rush. The vampire that had slid from the shutters was not rushing toward her brother, but savoring the moment.

Lacey looked at Sherree. Selfish. Silly. But Lacey felt a strange deep love for her. The kind of love, perhaps, that parents have: an unconditional love, for whoever and whatever their child turns out to be. Lacey liked it that Sherree had come back, had danced a little jig of joy because she had been a good person after all. Lacey liked the strength with which Sherree had tried to escape, even though that had let the vampire out of the shutters.

What strange lives these vampires led: half frozen by their own hibernation, but half frozen by the lack of available victims.

Perhaps all evil was like that.

Perhaps it lay in wait for you, lying behind the door, in back of the shutters, hidden by walls and strangers and habits . . . but it was there.

Perhaps you had only to say the words, and evil could begin growing, and filling every room and mind with its sick odor and its disgusting cloak.

I know the truth, thought Lacey. I understand the world. And what difference does it make? I will never get out there to tell anybody.

Lacey studied Bobby, whose magnificent muscular body had engineered many an athletic victory. Had Bobby learned anything from the night? It was hard to tell. With a person like Bobby, you tended not to look past the physical person to locate the emotional person. Bobby would always be able to hide behind his body, so to speak. He could put his muscles and his masculine beauty out front and nobody would know who was in back.

Zach, to whom appearances meant so much: Zach, expending so much energy trying not to be embarrassed or nervous or uncool. In a way she loved Zach most, because he was the most desperate to pull it all off. She wanted him to pull it all off. She wanted Zach to have it all, and not know how frail he really was.

Roxanne, who was not frail, and who did have it all, and who knew it. Lacey decided that after all, she liked Roxanne best, because Roxanne was toughest. Strong enough to rip nails out of floors, strong enough to herd scared kids down dark stairs.

Lacey admired strength. I won't have any ever again, thought Lacey. Once the vampire takes me, strength will be gone forever.

She studied Randy, although he was safe without her.

Randy, who was everything the vampire had accused him of. Dumb as ever: a sixteen-year-old showoff who didn't know when to stop. But Lacey loved him for wanting to be a hero. She loved him for being crushed when it turned out his bravery saved only himself. If all the world wanted to be a hero, perhaps evil would never come out from behind the shutters.

I just hope he doesn't drive too fast when they speed away from the mansion, thought Lacey. I just hope they catch Kevin and take him with them. They have to do that. My parents have to have one whole child.

"Take me," she said to the vampire.

In a businesslike way she said to the rest, "Hurry on. There's no time to waste. My brother is down there. Take him home with you. Get going."

Chapter 13

This time it was for real.

They would go.

She would stay.

The others touched Lacey. Stared. Rested a hand briefly on her shoulder. But they did not hug or kiss. They were too stunned. Too fearful.

"But we won't remember you!" cried Sherree. "I have to remember you! I want to be a better person. I want to have you to go by."

Her gift to me, thought Lacey. I accept. If she were permitted to remember, she would remember me, and be a better person for it.

But they won't remember. They will walk out that door and not remember. All their lives, as they go on in safety and joy, it will be because of me. And they won't remember.

Lacey thought of herself as dead, lying in a cemetery, but with a blank stone, because nobody remembered. She was just a granite slab to mow around.

She did not cry. She had made her decision. It

felt firm and right to her, though sad.

She thought of the days in which we honor the vanished: Memorial Day, Veterans' Day, Presidents' Day. I never honored anybody, thought Lacey. I just went to the sales at the department stores.

I forgot them. I live because they died. *And I forgot them.* As I will be forgotten. As I will forget myself.

Lacey felt that being forgotten was worse than anything.

To be good, and do right, and yet disappear with the rising sun.

Bobby cleared his throat. "Lacey?" he said.

She managed a smile.

"I wish we could go out. I always wanted to go out with you."

Lacey was amused. Bobby actually believed that it would make Lacey feel better to know that he, Bobby, had considered her as a date. Not asked, of course. Not actually phoned. But taken it into his mind.

"Thanks, Bobby," she said, being just a fraction sarcastic.

Athletic swing intact, Bobby turned to leave.

Roxanne whispered, "Oh, Lacey! I guess I should have volunteered. It's all on you. It's so unfair." She tried not to cry.

Lacey could have been mean. She could have said, Yes, you should have, you rotten person!

Lacey wanted to say it. But even though nobody would remember, and the words would be erased as if they had never been spoken, she did not say anything mean.

"It's okay, Roxanne," said Lacey kindly. "Just be sure you get Kevin."

Roxanne had a task to do now, and it strengthened her; Roxanne was a girl who needed a purpose. She moved quickly toward the door.

Zach did not get close to Lacey. He gave her a sort of salute. She understood that he was eager to forget; that Zach, too, knew he should have volunteered, should have fought, should have remained steadfast against this vampire. Zach was practically leaning down the stairs, getting himself out the dining room window, so ready to forget that it might not work for him; he might be the only one to remember.

What will be worse? thought Lacey. It will be terrible to forget . . . but to remember. To remember all that you could have done and didn't . . . perhaps that will be worst of all.

Randy gave her an awkward pat with his bunched fist, the way boys greet each other. It was hardly the motion for a date to give the girl he was leaving behind. He knew it after he'd done it, and was upset, and did not know what to do next.

He'll never know what to do next, thought Lacey. He'll be one of those people that's always a social nuisance. But he tried. He'll always try.

She hugged Randy, and only Randy.

Randy was deeply moved, even thrilled.

She was a human sacrifice who accepted him, Randy, for her last human touch in the world.

Zach was not leaning toward the door in order to forget. He was leaning in order to remember. Zach's well-ordered family used many Post-It notes, on refrigerator doors and medicine cabinet mirrors and car dashboards, so that they would forget nothing in their busy lives. He had, of course, a thin pad of adhesive note squares in his pocket and a tiny pencil, so he could jot down important thoughts and destinations.

To be sure he did not abandon Lacey here, Zach had written instructions to himself.

Call Police.

Call Fire Department.

Call Mr. and Mrs. James.

Lacey is in the Mall House alone. Get her out.

Zach would have been crushed to find how low an opinion of him Lacey had formed.

Sherree liked simple solutions.

When Sherree was depressed, she made no attempt to solve her problems. She just went shopping.

When Sherree felt less successful and less interesting than other girls in her class, she made no attempt to study harder or develop hobbies. She just slid her favorite CD into her sound system and danced.

She was not in a position to go shopping tonight.

Nor did dancing seem like a solution to Lacey's internment with the vampire.

There were only two other things on earth that interested Sherree: boys and cars.

The boys had been spectacularly unsuccessful at rescuing anybody.

So Sherree thought *car*.

She would drive the Land Rover right up the porch and into the house. A Land Rover was the kind of vehicle that could knock down walls, weak ones, at least, and this house was destined for that anyway. It would surely distract the vampire to have a car driving into his home. Sherree would lean on the horn and attract lots of attention and people would come and finish the rescue for her.

It would be very exciting.

Sherree had always wanted to drive in a demolition derby, and, of course, belonged to a family where the slightest scratch on a car sent them into frenzied phone calls to the body shop, so this was a childhood dream come true.

Randy had a different view of the situation. He had brought a video camera, and stupidly, left it in the Land Rover. But the point was, the camera was there and waiting for them. He was sure that vampires were afraid of having their pictures taken.

He would advance on them, holding his videocam like a shield before him, and film them and they would flee.

Lacey would be his forever.

Lacey.

How brave she was.

She could have been one of those pioneers, who, deciding to cross the Rocky Mountains come hell or high water, had pushed the family's belongings in a handcart, and carried the babies on her back, and brought with her the grain to plant the first garden.

No wonder the vampire was pleased that Lacey had accepted the offer.

She was the only one in the room worth having, even by a vampire's standards.

Randy thought about his and Lacey's future together. He didn't care what the vampire said; Randy would forget nothing. And Lacey would not forget, either; Randy would be her hero, and she would adore him.

Randy thought of the dates they would have, and the way she would look up to him.

Roxanne held the hammer back in her hand. She'd read many books where enemies attacked each other in various painful ways – often hurting them badly enough to cripple them for life. The vampire was now fully fleshed out. Roxanne would hurt him — so that he *never* recovered.

Roxanne pretended to walk toward the door.

She shifted over a little, though, getting closer to the vampire even as Randy was hugging Lacey good-bye.

Her hand tightened on the hammer.

She was wildly proud of herself. Violence! That was what would work. Lacey was being kind, but kindness, in the end, would only lead to her destruction. Roxanne would use what television had taught her to use: a weapon.

Bobby swaggered.

He tried to take up a lot of space. He flexed his arms and fingers as often as he could to warm up. He didn't like the fact that this heavy action he had in mind had been preceded by such weakness on his part, but there was nothing he could do about that now.

He had Lacey to save and he had revenge to take.

And he was, Bobby knew for sure, the only one with a workable plan.

He would rip the cloak off the vampire.

The cloak was obviously part of the creature, and in some way his powerful, protective part. And yet it was separate. The vampire liked to uncover only his teeth and his hands and parts of his face. Bobby would shred the thing.

Even if it did not destroy the vampire, which Bobby was sure it would, it would give everybody lots of time to run out while the vampire tried to save himself and wrap himself back up.

Strength and determination flew down Bobby's veins and arteries and coursed through his muscles. Bobby felt like a giant, a quarterback, a soldier for hire. There was nothing he could not do.

Lacey ran a hand down Randy's chest.

Randy's chest swelled with pride. He had never felt so strong and so needed. I'll save you, he thought, careful to give no hints. He must not let the vampire know what he was up to. The vampire might try to foil him. The vampire might even rush the "event" along, giving Randy little time to save Lacey.

Lacey put her head against Randy's chest, and Randy nearly melted. He was so distracted, he nearly forgot his master plan.

"Don't worry, Lacey," he whispered. "Everything will be all right. I promise."

Lacey looked up, gave him a gentle close-lipped smile, and stepped away from him.

The vampire's fingernails were weightless.

They scraped over Zach's clothing, dipped into his pocket and removed his notes.

"You won't need these outside," said the vampire softly.

He chuckled. He was enjoying himself.

Oh, it had been a night to remember, all right. But the one who would remember, the one who was having the most fun, the one who was playing the longest game, was the vampire.

Zach could not believe he had been noticed.

Had been stopped.

"Go," said the vampire to Zach, and the word was so intense, so meaningful, that Zach could do nothing else.

He went.

The doorway was open. It was possessed by nothing. Zach did not stumble, Zach did not falter, and his feet found the way in spite of the darkness.

* * *

Then the vampire caught Sherree's hand. Her clenched fist fell open at his touch and she whimpered when he took the car keys. "No," she blubbered. "See, I need the car keys. I took them from Randy because I need them."

"Don't worry," said the vampire. "Once you are out of the mansion, you will forget why you needed them. You'll hunt for a while, everybody feeling his pockets to see who has them."

The vampire, still holding Sherree's hand, tossed the car keys out the open tower window.

"Eventually," said the vampire, "you'll see them in the grass. You'll wonder why Randy dropped them there, and what took the five of you so long to see them."

Randy thought: How will I even be able to open the Land Rover? I have to have the keys!

He willed himself to remember that the keys had been thrown into the grass, so that he could find them quickly, open the car, grab the camera, race back inside, scare off the vampire before the vampire could . . .

"It would be a waste of your energy," explained the vampire. "Although you are welcome to try. We aren't afraid of having our pictures taken, it's just that we don't show up on film, Randy. So it's an ineffectual threat." The vampire smiled widely. His teeth hung cruelly and he scraped them along his chin, as if sharpening them. His eyes left Randy and traveled eagerly over Lacey.

"Time for you to go," said the vampire softly to

Sherree and to Randy, and Sherree and Randy found themselves going, obeying, as if they were possessions of the vampire in the same manner that the door had been a possession of the vampire.

The door was open.

They went through it.

Only Roxanne and Bobby stood between Lacey and the vampire now.

The vampire is horrible, thought Roxanne. He's horrible. He has no right to stage things like this, so we can't beat him back. But I have a hammer, and steel isn't stopped by vampires, steel isn't camera film or car keys, steel will break his bones.

Roxanne swung the hammer back, savoring the heft of it, looking forward to the crunch of bone when she hit the hideous creature. She threw herself forward. The hammer swung through the air and made contact with absolutely nothing.

There was nothing there.

She fell forward, her own velocity carrying her right into the vampire, and still there was nothing there but stinking evil. She fell onto the floor of the tower and the vampire gently retrieved the hammer from her hand.

How can he react so gently to us, thought Roxanne, when in a moment he will show total violence?

"It is my way," said the vampire to Roxanne, "to damage human bodies, but fortunately, humans cannot damage my body. It's time for you to go, Roxanne. There is the door."

She was on the floor.

His eyes fixed on her and his teeth leaned toward her and she scrabbled toward the door, not quite crawling, not quite getting up.

The vampire watched with satisfaction.

Bobby took advantage of the vampire's distraction and hurled himself at the vampire. His fingers wrapped solidly on the cloak and he ripped and tore with all his football player's strength.

And nothing happened.

He swung there, as he had swung in the doorway.

And through the hideous fibers of the rotting cloak he saw what would happen to Lacey.

"The cloak doesn't come off," explained the vampire. "You could rip for eternity, and you would just hang in the wind." The vampire walked toward the door and deposited Bobby on the other side. Bobby's fingers unwrapped. His feet found the first step. A queer wind blew him forward, escorting him down the steep stairs after the others.

Already his mind was vague, his thoughts muddy, his words slurred. "Hey, you guys," he said. Nobody turned to answer him. All five simply staggered down, and across, and found the window, and struggled to get out.

For them, the evening was over.

Chapter 14

When she was with Jordan, Ginny was usually acutely aware of her looks. In some ways, in fact, it was more relaxing not to be with Jordan. A boyfriend's presence demanded so much. Ginny had to worry about lipstick and hair and perfume and clothing and being funny and being sweet and being interesting and being . . .

Oh, it was exhausting.

She liked being in love, but she was also sort of looking forward to the time when she would not be in love, when it would be rather dull and ordinary and she would not have to pour so much energy into this.

It was most odd to have been in a car together, in the dark, unaware of Jordan. She knew he was there, of course. And yet she did not look at him. Not when they drove up to the horrible old house. Not when they got out of the car. Not when they moved over the ground toward the shadowed building.

145

Her eyes seemed caught inside the cylinder of a kaleidoscope. She could look nowhere except down into the pattern, into the tumbling, falling, changing colors.

Ginny felt herself and her life tumble, fall, and change, and yet there were no colors.

There was only texture, and all of it black. First it was a square of velvet, and then it was the bottom of a cave. It whirled and turned and became moss and then silk, caked with mud.

Its curving approach was the most exciting thing Ginny had ever seen, and the most frightening.

She wanted to run and yet the only direction her feet took was directly into it.

A smell like a cesspool filled her head.

She looked up and saw the kaleidoscope of meshing white teeth.

Usually Jordan could think of nothing but Ginny. Her shape, her scent, her laugh, her teasing, her hair . . . but he had lost that. Ginny receded from his mind, as if she had set off on some long unknown journey, and they would meet again years from now.

Jordan knew that his girlfriend was right there, only a few feet from him, and yet he did not think about her.

He saw nothing but that building: that sagging porch, those boarded-up windows, that tilted tower, those shining slates.

But there was no moon. There were no stars.

There were no streetlights. What could shine on the roof? What was he seeing?

It was entirely dark, and yet it gleamed.

Jordan shuddered, suddenly afraid, and that outraged him, because Jordan did not believe in fear. If you had the proper attitude, you controlled any foolish emotion like that.

Fear possessed him.

Fear had actually become Jordan, like race or height.

He wanted to hang onto something, to steady himself. He wanted to go back to the car, but the only direction his body seemed to know was forward.

The porch, he thought, I'll hang onto the porch.

He tried to steer his feet to the porch, as if, beneath that underhang of roof and gutter he would be safe from the descending blackness.

The dark was incredibly thick, as if it knew more than Jordan ever would. The darkness took on life and smothered Ginny.

There was no time for thought, which was lucky, because Jordan could formulate no thoughts about what was happening. He tackled Ginny, as if they were football players. The two of them smacked the ground, and the blackness curled away from them, because they were two, and the vampire could take only one at a time.

The vampire simply smiled. There were plenty more. No need to fret over a lost victim.

* * *

It was Zach who came first through the window. Zach whose shivering hands pushed at the plywood one more time, and pried open a slot through which he could crawl.

He was outside.

He felt that his whole life had been a preparation for this moment: that this was the first time in his sixteen years he had truly breathed. How wonderful the oxygen was. How clear the night. How good he felt. How strong and intelligent. Zach smiled, and he could even feel his teeth: how straight and white and —

Teeth.

The word gave him a shudder, but he did not know why.

He stood on the porch trying to think, but thoughts did not fill his brain the way they normally did. He felt empty. As if something had siphoned him off.

Notes, thought Zach. I took notes. He found the little pad of Post-Its he always carried, and the stub of a pencil. He held the tiny pages up to read, but the top one was blank.

Blank, thought Zach. I need oxygen, he thought next.

Get off the porch, he told himself. Get out of this place. Breathe deep. Relax. Calm. Then figure out the next step.

The vampire of the shutters decided next on the little girl racing away from the car tucked among the dead trees. The vampire loved dead trees. Yes, this really was a wonderful location. He greatly regretted that his home was vanishing under the bulldozers. He swooped upward for a moment, and smiled, preparing for the final, the precious, the wonderful descent.

Sherree staggered right into Zach as she climbed out the dining room window. "Zach!" she said, as if he were the last person on earth she would have expected to run into.

They stared at each other. "Hi, Sherree," said Zach.

"I'm here with Bobby," she said.

"I remember," he said, and they beamed at each other. They were delighted to possess a fact. A tiny piece of memory.

"We're in a hurry," said Sherree. "I have to get the car. I have to drive somewhere. I'm sure that — I think that — I know that — "

But she was not sure. She could not think. She did not know.

She and Zach frowned at each other and examined each other's frowns, as if peeling away the wrinkles might lead to explanations.

The policewoman went inside Dunkin Donuts.

She sipped her coffee slowly.

She nibbled at her jelly doughnut, making it last.

No static came from her strapped-on radio. No stations were busy. No action was occurring anywhere: not in the police department, not in the fire department, not in the ambulance department.

The evening was dead.

Darkness swarmed like a million wasps wanting to nest in her hair.

Mardee screamed.

Fingers touched her skin.

Damp stinking air, as if it had life and swamp breath, crawled down her neck.

Mardee leaped forward with more strength than she had known she possessed and grabbed hold of Kevin's belt. Kevin, yelling, "Lace! Lace!" reached back without slowing down and yanked Mardee along with him.

There was a weird, sick moment in which they seemed suspended, as if something had caught them.

And then Kevin broke free, and took Mardee forward with him.

Zach reached the railing of the wide steps down off the porch. Another hand was there before him. It was a young man, but nobody Zach knew.

Police? thought Zach. He didn't want to get in any trouble. Whose idea had it been to party at the Mall House anyway? Stupid idea. Zach could not imagine why they had come. He could not imagine why they were leaving, either.

His hand gripped the banister only inches away from that other hand. The fingers faced opposite directions. The other hand was coming in, as Zach was going out.

The young man said, "I'm looking for Ginny's little brother."

Zach and Sherree stared at him. Do we know somebody named Ginny? thought Zach. I know I don't know anybody named Ginny. Who's here, anyway? Zach turned around to look. Randy, he thought. Bobby, he thought. Who else?

"Ginny's little brother?" repeated the man. "Did he crash the party? Is he in there with you?"

Sherree said slowly, "Somebody crashed the party. I remember that . . . somebody . . . but . . . I don't think it was Ginny's little brother."

It was Lacey's little brother who raced up on the porch. Zach couldn't think of the kid's name. He wasn't so much of a dwindle-head as his sister, but still Zach had never had much use for him.

"My sister!" shouted the kid.

Right behind him came Bobby's little sister, Mardee. Zach didn't have a whole lot of use for Mardee, either. In fact, Zach was beginning to feel quite annoyed that he was spending a perfectly good weekend in the company of so many dwindle-heads.

The porch filled up.

The party had come outside.

Roxanne was there, and Randy and Bobby.

An older teenage girl Zach didn't know joined the guy looking for a kid brother.

The place looked like an airport. Everybody racing around trying to find the right gate. They raced around the porch instead. They had the same mental franticness of lost passengers. Where's my plane, where's my luggage, who's meeting me, where did we leave the car, didn't I have my coat with me?

Zach had never been to a farm and never seen live farm animals, but he had once read the phrase "running around like a chicken with its head cut off." That sentence alone was enough to keep Zach from ever going near a farm, let alone having chickens. What kind of animal ran around after its head had been cut off? And why would you want to cut off its head anyway?

But that's what they behaved like.

Chickens with their heads cut off.

Nine people, darting left, darting right, running down the porch stairs, running back up, clutching each other, barging into each other.

You'd think our heads were cut off, thought Zach.

It was not their heads that had been cut off, of course. Just their memories. To have no memory was deeply confusing. They did not know where they were going nor where they had come from. They did not know what to do next nor with whom to do it.

And they did not, this confused, blank-minded crowd of nine, look up at the sky.

Even Ginny had lost sight of the sky, caught up with Jordan and these people circling the porch steps like birds at a feeder.

* * *

It is true that there is safety in numbers.

The vampire of the shutters could not penetrate so sturdy a crowd.

He had taken time with his descent, revelling in the silly human mob behavior. Humans were so predictable. They lost their heads and what did they do? They ran back and forth, as if they thought they would find their thoughts lying on one side of the lawn or the other.

The vampire slid like a migrating bird from one side of the sky to another. Each human attracted him in its own way. Each had a certain something that made the human appealing.

Which would he take?

How would the "event" progress?

It was wonderful to be awake. To have his mind active, to feel his teeth growing, preparing themselves. To have his cloak sift through the night air, instead of being trapped indoors as he had been for so very, very long. The vampire felt strong and able, and he felt eager and excited.

For several minutes he simply watched. If they had looked up they would have seen his smile. It was quite distinctive.

But humans were concerned only with each other. They knew so pathetically little of the night. They knew nothing of stars, or darkness, or shadows. In fact, they tried to pretend the night was not there. They turned on lights the instant there was the slightest suggestion of night in the sky. As if night were the enemy.

Night was a friend.

To me, at least, thought the vampire.

He waited patiently for one of the pack to wander from the rest, to be sufficiently in shadow that nobody would see the vampire's descent.

"I was supposed to be doing something," said Randy nervously. He was twitching, patting himself, as if a clue would stick out from his shirt pocket.

"Going home, probably," said Ginny sharply. "We were out hunting for my brother. My parents are crazy with worry."

"We'll give you a ride," said Jordan. "Everybody pile in."

Sherree loved a crowded car. "We can't possibly all fit," she said, giggling. Her parents were very stern on seat belt use. There would be twice as many people as there were belts. "I'll sit on laps," said Sherree eagerly, and just as eagerly, both Bobby and Zach volunteered their laps.

Randy stood on the bottom porch step, looking around. "I forgot something," he said, feeling thick and stupid.

"Your car," said Jordan, pointing. "You guys are pathetic. I mean, what did you think was going to happen here anyway?"

"We were going to make it happen," said Randy. He remembered what he had forgotten. His car keys. He patted his pockets again.

"I took them," said Sherree, patting herself. But she had no pockets, and she was holding no keys.

The night seemed curiously romantic to Mardee. Kevin seemed unexpectedly strong and attractive.

She had a sense of being interrupted, as if they had been doing something fascinating and worth repeating. She touched Kevin's shoulder as if she were afraid of it, and he caught his breath as if he were afraid of her touch, too; as if it would lead to something.

"Let's not go with them," whispered Mardee.

Kevin nodded. "We walked over, we'll walk back."

They clasped each other's waists.

A molecule of memory hit Kevin. "Wait," he said to the others. "My sister. Lacey. Wasn't she with you?"

"That dwindle-head," muttered Zach. But he did not say it loud enough for the dwindle-head's brother to hear. And the moment he called her that, he felt guilty. And wrong.

As if he knew better than to say a thing like that.

He caught Sherree glaring at him. "She is not," said Sherree sharply.

"I know," said Zach guiltily. But he did not know why he felt guilty nor why he knew that Lacey was not a dwindle-head. He looked up at the mansion.

It stood dark and formless in the night.

He knew its roof was a sharp pattern of angles and dips, of slate and tower. He knew because —

I fell off that tower! thought Zach. I — I — I —

But how could he have fallen off that tower? He'd have been killed if he'd fallen from that height.

Weird, thought Zach. We must really have partied. Zach shook his head, to clear it, but it did not clear. Something in his thoughts remained murky and dulled.

Lacey's brother said, "Are you sure Lacey isn't with you?"

Everybody looked around. Lacey did not seem to be there.

"She must have left early," said Ginny. "Making her the only smart one in the group." Ginny pointed to the backseat and began herding passengers into Jordan's car. They got in slowly.

Lacey? thought Roxanne.

Lacey? wondered Bobby.

Lacey?

But their thoughts did not come clear.

They took no action.

They formed no response.

One by one, they got in Jordan's car, giggling, because they were as crowded as clowns, and it was fun.

One by one the victims that had escaped the first vampire also moved out of reach of the second vampire.

The vampire of the shutters was furious.

Fury made his teeth sharper and his hunger more urgent.

He retreated. Height helped him stay calm. Height gave him the velocity he would need for a surprise attack.

The car was just too crowded, and Mardee was feeling too young and too romantic to wedge herself into that group. "Let's walk," she reminded Kevin, and they wrapped arms around each other's waists and moved past the station wagon and out toward the road.

"We had a good time, didn't we?" said Kevin. He felt confused, saying that because he could no longer remember what kind of time they had had. But Mardee squeezed him tighter and he no longer cared, either. He was happy. He didn't look back. He didn't remember the building only yards behind him, he didn't remember the screams only moments earlier, and he didn't remember the threat that had nearly peeled Mardee from his side.

He didn't remember his sister, Lacey, at all.

The vampire saw movement deep in the dead trees. A door opening, and a head peering out. Another human. A human who had previously been hidden in the shadows. Another human caught in curiosity, that strange human weakness.

The vampire knew immediately that this human was different. This was a human who used the dark. This was a human within whom there was also an element of darkness. The vampire enjoyed the innocence of some of his victims, but there was a certain pleasure also in a victim who had had victims of his own.

This was not a clean nor an attractive human.

But the vampire of the shutters had no standards in that regard.

Slowly his black folds enveloped the car thief.

In the starless, moonless night there was no sound, no sight.

Only a slow suffocation.

Chapter 15

Lacey had not been thinking of Randy when she put her arms around him. She had been interested exclusively in the contents of Randy's shirt pocket. The little toys with which Randy had played all evening. The objects he had caressed, like worry beads, to pull himself together. In the end, all six teenagers had pulled together, but memory would defeat them.

Loss of memory, that is.

Lacey, however, would suffer no such loss. Not until afterward.

Right now, in this tower, facing this vampire, the situation was all too clear.

One by one, the vampire dismissed her five companions. Soul by soul, the room contained less humankind, and more evil. How reluctant the vampire was to let them go. After all, when would he again have such a lovely situation? The rules by which he lived were not simple.

But the rules by which I live, thought Lacey, are not simple, either.

I refuse to be his next event. And that's it. I will direct my life and it will go on the way I choose. Not the way he chooses. So there!

The vampire was too busy playing games with the other five to pick up on her thoughts. Lacey took a small slow step to the center of the room while the vampire was busy collecting Zach's notes. She took a second, equally slow step while the vampire was tossing the car keys out the window.

Her hand was tight on the tiny object she had taken from Randy's pocket.

The timing had to be exact.

Her feet were at the edge of the nest that Roxanne had exposed. She did not change position again. Instead she inched her foot forward, over the torn wooden strips, until she could tell that half her foot was in the air, poised over the vampire's lair.

The vampire took his time. His eyes glittered as each potential victim passed, untouched, through the door.

Lacey never took her eyes off the vampire.

There was no point in watching the others. There was no point in anything now, except her plan.

For Zach had been right, after all, when hours ago he had called for an analysis of the vampire's weaknesses. Lacey knew one. Roxanne had exposed it.

Whatever this opening was in the floor . . . this cell . . . this tomb . . . this grave . . . he had to have it. When Roxanne had invaded the nest, the vampire's power had vanished. He had disappeared from the room and from their hearts and souls as if he had never been.

He had, unluckily, been lurking down the stairs, and just as Randy had said would happen, the vampire blocked their escape.

But Zach was correct. There was weakness. The vampire had to have his nest. If Lacey destroyed it, he would have to waft away, or dematerialize, or whatever it is that vampires do.

The other five teenagers were gone. The sound of their footsteps dwindled away. The sound of their guilty voices disappeared.

The vampire turned with a sweet smile. His teeth were not showing. He said, "Do not be afraid, my dear."

"I'm not," said Lacey loftily. But she was.

"And do not waste time tipping yourself over into my home. I will merely join you." His cloak came first and she shuddered. That made him smile. Now his teeth sprouted.

How pathetic and unlikely her plan seemed in sight of those teeth.

"You could scream," said the vampire.

She remembered that he liked screams. Perhaps if she screamed, the others, who must by now be climbing out the dining room window, would remember her long enough to do something.

"No," said the vampire courteously. "That is not a possibility. The human brain is shallow. It retains nothing for long. No lesson, no experience, leaves a human with lasting knowledge. Sad," whispered the vampire, coming closer, "but true." His breath encircled her and she could not breathe.

"However," said the vampire, "it works to my advantage."

Lacey fell into his nest.

The stench of it, the oily horror of it, practically ate through her mind. I won't be able to finish! thought Lacey. I won't have enough oxygen to finish.

Was there even enough oxygen to do what she needed to do?

Lacey stared up into the descending folds of the vampire's cloak and with her hidden hand, flicked the lighter. There was enough oxygen.

The vampire could control many of the laws of nature.

Gravity could be his, if he chose.

But not fire.

The house was old. Very old. And very dry.

The wood was tinder, waiting for fire. The splinters Roxanne had torn up turned into leaping screaming golden flames. The vampire retreated. He screamed, "You'll burn up yourself!"

Lacey got out, fanning the fire with the edge of the vampire's own cloak. "Burn!" she shouted at the fire. "Burn!"

The flame ate the nest and leaned forward, as if to begin on the hem of the vampire's cloak.

The vampire put out his crinkled hand, like used aluminum foil, and retreated to the corner of the tower. "You can't do this!" he screamed.

"I already have," she pointed out. "Go ahead and scream. I don't mind. I like the sound of a vampire screaming."

The vampire's mouth was wide open, wide, wide, wide. And yet its teeth were of no consequence. It could only scream. "My home!" it screamed. "You can't destroy my home. I will have nowhere to go when dawn arrives."

"Your weakness," said Lacey. She bared her own teeth: her small, square, even, white teeth. Her human teeth. She turned them into a smile of triumph.

"You'll suffocate!" he warned.

"I'd rather take my chances with smoke than teeth."

Whatever nesting material lay in the hollow between the floor joists had turned to ash. The room filled with smoke. Lacey could not go out the windows, because the flames, desperate for oxygen to eat, the way the vampire had been desperate for blood, were reaching through the windows.

In school, home of the frequent fire drill, they told you to get down on the floor in case of fire: There you would find better air.

How laughable.

Down on the floor was the swamp gas of the vampires.

But she obeyed the school directive she had heard three or four times a year since kindergarten.

Stop, drop, and roll!

How many times had they had to crayon posters for Fire Prevention Week?

Stop, drop, and roll!

Lacey heard the vampire screaming. Her own lungs were starved for air, her eyes burning with heat. She crawled to the door. Would it be blocked? Would the vampire have taken possession of it again, once the other five were safely out and on their way?

Stop, drop, and roll.

Lacey rolled to the door. The flames engulfed the floor as if the fire were chasing her feet.

The doorway was open.

The vampire had not taken possession of it.

He had trusted her.

Lacey actually smiled.

A creature that dealt in evil trusted a human who dealt in good. The vampire had believed in Lacey's volunteering. The vampire had assumed along with volunteering would come cooperation and an assortment of screams.

He had not expected any double-dealing from Lacey James, who was good.

But sometimes, in tight corners, when your back is against the wall and the world is against you, you have to fight back in unexpected ways.

Lacey rolled down the stairs to get away from the smoke and the flames and felt nothing on the way down: no pain, no bruises, no fear. And most of all, no pursuit. For the vampire could not get through the sheet of flames that rose up between his victim and himself. She got up and ran down the lower flight, found the abandoned dining room, felt along the walls until she found the window.

Coughing, lungs hurting, she climbed out onto the porch and staggered onto the lawn.

There was nobody around. No Bobby, no Zach. No Sherree, no Roxanne. No Randy. No friends at all.

A car was driving away. In the fading darkness she saw its red taillights.

Ashes from the burning tower flew into the air and spun in circles, like tiny tornadoes. The wind carried them, and dropped them into the huge pile of dead trees. The dry hemlocks caught fire and became a ball of flame as big as the Mall House itself. So much for the Land Rover, thought Lacey.

She ran across the yard. Out what had once been a gate, what had once been a driveway.

She raced across what was still a road.

The house screamed. Or was it the house? Could a house scream?

Lacey turned to stare. The Mall House was caving in.

For one moment the tower was a complete circle of fire, and then it fell, stumbling over the rest of the roof and falling to the ground. Lacey put her hands over her hair, as if it could shield her from catching fire, and ran farther, putting the fireblock of pavement between herself and the inferno.

On the other side of the street stood her brother. Her little brother, Kevin! "Kevin?" said Lacey, astonished. "What are you doing here?"

"What are *you* doing here?" said Kevin, of course.

Lacey did not know the girl with him. What an

odd world it was. She had never dreamed her brother liked girls. But then, she had never dreamed that vampires really existed, either. Let alone in her town. In her life. Among the houses and streets of her world.

From far away she heard a siren.

Somebody had alerted the fire department.

Lacey looked back at the flames and the collapsing walls. Sirens screamed louder than victims. Sparks shot into the sky, and fell back, and the rest of the house turned into one vast bonfire.

The only smell in the night was the rich smoky burning of wood.

"Keep walking," said Lacey, and the three kept walking. Whatever mechanism had taken memory from the others had not worked on Lacey. Not yet, at least. In her mind, she turned over what had happened.

The road was full of shadows, but none of them descended. They were shadows of other trees, other buildings. But not shadows of other worlds. The vampires had lost their nests: lost their floors and ceilings, shutters and towers and mansion.

Had they lost their power, too?

Or could they drift, unseen, through the sky before the coming of dawn?

Could they find another hole? An open coffin? A mausoleum with a broken door?

Or had they been destroyed?

They were evil, thought Lacey James. I do not think evil can be destroyed. Only subdued for a time.

"Hi," said the girl with Kevin. "I'm Mardee. Bobby's sister. I'm glad to meet you."

Lacey said hi.

A squad car driven by a policewoman took the corner at top speed. The tires screamed. The night, in fact, was full of screams.

But not mine, thought Lacey. I did not scream. I won.

And instead of screaming, Lacey James laughed.

For she had looked at her watch. It was not even midnight. All this had happened in so few hours it was not even a new day.

"Thought you were spending the night with somebody," said Kevin.

"Changed my mind," said Lacey.

Memory faded. Lacey and Kevin and Mardee walked along the road, and turned up the hill, and forgot the mansion behind them, the shadows, and the screams.

The hard-learned lessons, the heroism, and the sacrifices were gone as if they had never been.

And the shadows that were the vampires hung in the sky, and departed, desperate, for they had only a few hours until dawn, only a few hours in which to find another nest.

But usually, for a vampire, a few hours is enough.

About the Author

CAROLINE B. COONEY lives in a small seacoast village in Connecticut, with three children and two pianos. She writes every day on a word processor and then goes for a long walk down the beach to figure out what she's going to write the following day. She has written about thirty-six books for young people including *The Cheerleader* and *The Return of the Vampire*, and *The Perfume*. She also plays the piano for the school music programs, is learning jazz, reads a mystery novel a night, and does a lot of embroidery.